D0920904

THE
TWELFTH COIN

F I N D E R S

by

Kimberly Erjavac

Illustrations by Linda Kritz

Beach Street Park Publishing

Library of Congress Control Number: 20561590202
ISBN 978-1-949111-00-2

Printed in the United States of America
First printing, first edition October 2018

To my mom, Tina Lomelin,
who taught her girls to work hard and follow their dreams.
I love you, Mom!

Contents

Acknowledgements

A special thanks to John Erjavac, without whom there would be no story.

When I began this writing journey my family could not have been more encouraging. So it is with great love and appreciation that I acknowledge Kristen Brock, Karen, Jeff, Claudia and Claire Crampton, Gayle and Mike McMurry, Amy, Stanley, Sam and Ben Erjavac. As the project unfolded, I searched for someone who could convey the story through images and was fortunate that my friend, advocate and artist extraordinaire, Linda Kritz, had the vision and talent to create the artwork that proceeds each chapter, for which I am eternally grateful. From the rough draft to the finished copy, no one could have been more selfless than my dear friend Kathi Shatzel in her willingness to read, reread, offer guidance and inspire, a generosity I hope to someday reciprocate. When the first draft was complete, the initial edit was performed by Kaitlin Olson, who made transforming my manuscript into a novel a very special experience. No one influenced how the story was to be told more than Jessi Shakarian, taking on the role of story editor and teacher. Words cannot describe how grateful I am for her help. After immersing myself into the subject of Physics, I was blessed to have John Canavan as a time travel consultant who offered keen insight and guidance. I could always count on Charles Carney, Allyn Warner, Sarah Rustam and Mary Miller for their direction and suggestions when I needed it. I found a kindred spirit when Mary Keyes entered the project and look forward to our next phase of working together. My gratitude goes out to contributing editors, Judy Henderson, Stephanie Parent, Deborah Dove who helped fine tune the material. Thank you to Allen Ruby for cover graphic design and interior formatting by Polgarus Studio. No one (other than me) has read the manuscript more times than Patti Smith. Her generosity of time and spirit has been a blessing. My appreciation goes out to all of those who gave feedback after reading advance reader copies, Cathy Malatesta, Jeffrey Kravitz, Marisa Cuccinello, Michelle Foster, Sharon Alfers, Kristina Walker, William Rehn, Melinda Anderson, PJ Loonam, Chelsea Davidson, Jack Mosley, Noelleen Westcombe, Amy Brusca, Kai Matsumoto, Nuala Giffon, and Kaitlyn Keyes.

Finally, to all of my clients and co-workers. Your unwavering support and encouragement helped me reach the finish line. Thank you!

PROLOGUE

Charlottesville, Virginia - December 1942

A crowd began to gather around the body lying in the street. Professor Paul Osborne stood transfixed, until a jolt from someone rushing to the scene pushed him forward. He wrenched his eyes away and, hiding behind his upturned collar, he started for home.

Was it a coincidence that his adversary, Thurman Miller, was struck by a car only a few feet in front of him? The professor raked his fingers through his graying hair as he picked up his pace. He knew the hit and run was no accident. He and Miller had both met with government officials, and were informed of a nuclear attack Germany was planning against the United States. The government expected to use the technology he and Miller were developing as a means of protection, notifying each of them to hand everything over or face the consequences.

"Your work is no longer your own, it belongs to the United States of America," is how the professor recalled them putting it.

Miller vowed never to share his findings with the professor or the government. That pledge left him facedown on the pavement. The professor stopped at the corner, looking both ways to ensure he didn't meet the same demise.

Sirens from the approaching ambulance grew louder. The professor stepped off the curb, barely noticing the wet snow that seeped into his worn loafers. Beads of sweat formed around his brow as he broke into a run. His apartment was only a few blocks from the university, but the faster he ran, the farther away it seemed. He finally reached the stairs, frantically searching his pockets for his keys, when the door flung open from the other side. He jumped as he saw his wife.

"Zorrie, what are you doing?" He pushed his way in, glancing over his shoulder to make sure no one had followed him. "I told you not to open the door for anyone."

"But I saw you through the peephole," she replied, as she closed the door behind them.

"I said for anyone," he shouted as he hurried to the front window and closed the curtains. "That includes me!"

The professor tugged at the collar of his sweat-soaked shirt, finding it difficult to breathe. From the small opening between the curtains he peered out, realizing that sooner or later they would find him. He couldn't spend his days fearing for the lives of his wife and son.

He had no choice. He must give the government what they wanted, but he would insist on one condition. They must allow him to see his project through to completion. Then, and only then, would he hand over all that he had developed. If they wanted the capability to alter the past, they were going to have to wait. The enormous hurdles he still faced could take years to overcome. That would give him plenty of time to devise a plan to keep them from stealing his life's work.

Two months later…

A gust of cold air blew through the open door of the generator room at the far end of the university. Professor Osborne looked beyond the ten scientists huddled around the table in the middle of the room and focused on George Cannon, the government representative leaning against the wall. The professor's blood boiled at the sight of him.

"Get that door locked," Professor Osborne snapped at his assistant Gordon.

Gordon hurried down the narrow pathway. "Today's the day," he whispered to himself. For years, Gordon had shared the professor's aspirations of creating a device that would give them the power to time travel. "This most definitely is the day!" he said as he smiled, pushing the door closed and securing the latch.

He returned to the small room that was dimly lit by three hanging lamps. The wood beams that stretched along the high ceiling were cluttered with bus bars and wires. A small furnace in the corner made the room hot and stuffy.

Professor Osborne parted the group of his colleagues as he walked over to the table where a large tray held twelve empty coin molds. Mounted to the floor were twelve solenoids, resembling miniature chimneys with a band stretched across the opening of each one. He made sure that the lever secured to the pole was in the off position before pulling down the straps and attaching them to the conductors on the solenoids.

Hanford, the eldest of the scientists in the room, slowly bent down and opened his case. "I brought the steering mechanism," he announced, showing everyone a rectangular piece of wood with two clock faces inset alongside gauges and meters.

"Remember, all discoveries achieved during this confidential collaboration will belong exclusively to the United States government," George announced, eyeing the old man as he shuffled over to the professor.

Professor Osborne took the steering device and examined it, while mumbling his discontent with George's statement.

"Professor, let me remind you," George said, glaring at the professor, "it was I who assembled this group of great minds to assist in expediting this project."

The professor ignored George's comment and turned to his assistant. "Is the copper ready?"

Gordon opened the door to the furnace and checked the cup-shaped crucible of melted copper. "Yes, sir," he replied eagerly.

"Ivan, do you have it?" the professor asked one of his fellow scientists.

Ivan was a star in the physics community. His studies using gravitational fields to slow time had gained him much recognition among scientific circles. His attempt to reignite the Enlightenment movement was also picking up steam, with Ivan touting his "Dare to Think" speech to anyone who would listen.

Ivan held out a wooden box that was a little larger than a deck of cards. "Yes, I've named it Nanostatic Fusion."

Professor Osborne noticed the carving on the lid was of an atom with its nucleus the shape an hourglass, the new symbol for Enlightenment. He removed the top of the box, revealing twelve mechanisms inside resembling tiny balls that had been flattened. All had a smooth coating except one, which was larger than the rest, with slits cut into its outer layer.

"Outstanding," the professor said, staring into the box. He picked up a pair of tweezers and bowed slightly as he handed them to Ivan. "You may have the honor."

Ivan placed a mechanism into each mold until eleven were distributed. He then reached for the larger one, and looked up at the professor before positioning it in the last empty mold.

Professor Osborne's heart raced as he watched, knowing that this Nanostatic Fusion was essential for the coins to work. He had spent his lifetime searching for something that could provide the energy he needed, only to find it now, while being observed by the government official waiting to confiscate his dream.

"We will be following the sequence discussed in our last meeting," The professor stated. "The dies to create both the front and back sides of the pennies are in the coin press. It is imperative that the coins are placed in the press before the copper fully hardens. Are there any questions?"

"No," the others replied.

"All right Gordon, fill the coin molds," the professor instructed.

Gordon reached into the furnace with large tongs and closed them around the crucible. Slowly moving toward the table, he carefully trickled the molten copper into the molds. Everyone watched as Ivan's mechanisms were covered by the hot liquid.

"Use a steady hand now," the professor said.

Gordon cautiously placed a mold on the bands atop each solenoid.

"These solenoids will produce strong electromagnetic fields," the professor explained. "In combination with the Nanostatic Fusion reaction, we will attempt to infuse the coins with continuous energy."

"Something that has never been done," Ivan added.

The professor caught Ivan's eye. They both knew they were on the brink of an extraordinary discovery, and there was no room for error. If they lost control of the power they were attempting to harness, it would result in an explosion that would take out half of the university. The professor looked at George, who was still leaning against the wall. He had half a mind to sabotage the project and prevent the government from ever getting their hands on his work.

NO! he thought. He was on the verge of accomplishing his dream and was not about to send it up in smoke. He would see this through, vowing that if they were successful in creating the coins, he would find a way to get them back from the government. The coins were rightfully his, and he would not rest until he had sole possession of them.

The professor glanced at the faces staring back at him. "Get the generator going," he told his assistant.

Gordon left the room, and it wasn't long before the intensifying sound of the generator motor became as loud as a jet plane engine.

"Send me some juice," the professor called out. "Start with a thousand amps. We're going to bring it up slowly."

There was a tapping sound overhead as the current made its way through the connectors to the bus bars. The professor pulled the lever attached to the pole. Everyone watched intently as energy flowed down the strap to the conductors.

"Ease it up to five thousand amps," Professor Osborne yelled to be heard over the generator. "Not too fast now, we need to hold the field stable."

No one's eyes moved from the solenoids.

"We're at five, Professor," Gordon called back.

"Okay, keep it going," the professor replied.

The assistant complied, slowly increasing the current.

"Six…seven… eight," Gordon shouted. Eight was as high as they had gone during tests they had conducted, and he waited for instruction to go further.

"Get us up to ten and hold it," the professor yelled back, wondering if their configuration could withstand such power.

Gordon resumed. "Eight and a half… nine… nine and a half."

The lights overhead flickered, and the table began to tremble.

"Ten!" Gordon shouted.

The twelve solenoids standing like smokestacks were turning bright orange and churning out toxic fumes, making it difficult to breathe. Everyone backed away, coughing and rubbing their burning eyes. The room was filling with smoke, and someone grabbed the fire extinguisher from the wall, aiming it at the solenoids.

"NO!" the professor howled, waving his arms.

"Ten!" Gordon repeated.

At that moment, bulbs from two of the overhead lamps burst, sending glass showering down on the scientists. There was a high-pitched ringing noise, so loud the professor could barely hear the snap of the breakers tripping.

"Cut the power!" he shouted. "Cut the power!"

The generator waned as everyone slowly raised their heads, brushing the glass from their shoulders. Gordon rushed into the room. By the light of the remaining lamp, he saw the shocked expressions on the faces of those in attendance.

"Check the coins," the professor called to him.

Gordon used the tongs to pull the coin molds from the glowing coils. "They've already cooled."

"Quickly! Bring them over to the coin press," the professor yelled. "We have to make the impression in the copper before they harden."

One by one, the eleven blanks emerged from the coin press, yielding perfect 1943 copper pennies. Those in the room passed the coins amongst themselves before inserting each one into a stone plaque. The blank with the larger mechanism was saved for last. It would be the twelfth coin, the master coin.

The professor's hands shook and he felt as though his heart was going to pound out of his chest as he put the final blank onto the coin press, pulling the lever. He slowly removed the coin and examined the flawless penny before inserting it into the top slot of the plaque.

Professor Paul Osborne stood tall, looking at the others, some of whom still seemed traumatized by the experience. He took a deep breath, and with his hands still trembling he lifted the plaque.

"It is complete," he announced. He breathed deeply once again. "Of course they must be tested, but I believe we have just created twelve coins that can change the world."

PART ONE

CHAPTER ONE

HAPPY BIRTHDAY

Carly

Calabasas, California. Seventy-some-odd years later…

Carly peered through her hair at Kevin's empty plate. Her eyes traveled down the picnic table, noticing no one else had finished. There was practically an entire steak in front of her dad, Sam, and her brother Ben was working on his. Bill was still eating as well, but she cut him some slack, since it was his birthday barbeque. Bill's wife, Sharon, had already pushed away from the table. Then of course there was Zack, who dove in for another heaping spoonful of potato salad. *This dinner will never end*, Carly thought. Her father caught her eye, as if he read her mind. She sighed, letting her head drop back on the chair.

All her dad had talked about for the past few days was this birthday party and the trip both families would be taking the following day. Even her brother seemed excited, if you could call it that. Since he quit the track team and broke up with his longtime girlfriend, Francesca, which in Carly's opinion were both big mistakes, saying Ben was excited about anything would be an overstatement. It didn't help that he had chosen to go the way of his father, preferring to do anything but stay home. Lately, half of his time had been spent with a guitar in his hands at band rehearsal, and the other half hanging out with Zack, which was another big mistake.

Carly noticed Zack still cramming food in his mouth and rolled her eyes. *Great! Stuck in a condo next to this dolt for my entire spring break; some vacation!*

"Thank you for the great birthday dinner," Bill said rubbing his belly.

"It's not over yet," Sharon said. "We still have cake."

Carly held back a painful moan.

"I don't know where I'll put it—I'm stuffed." Bill looked around his backyard. "What a perfect evening. It was a night just like tonight that my father gave me his watch." He leaned back and pulled a gold watch on a chain from his pocket.

"Not again!" Zack begged. "You tell this story every year."

"Yeah, Dad," Kevin added.

Bill ignored his sons and opened his watch to reveal a 1943 copper penny mounted on the inside of the cover. The penny, which he'd named The Lincoln, was his pride and joy. Neither Zack nor Kevin had ever seen the coin separate from the watch, nor had they seen the watch separate from their dad. The boys joked that he probably slept with it, and he did.

Bill stared at The Lincoln and explained, "During World War II, the government was conserving copper to use for ammunition. That's the reason the 1943 pennies were made from steel. During the pressing of those steel coins, there were twelve copper blanks in the machine that were pressed by mistake. Which makes this 1943 copper penny one of the rarest coins in the world."

"Really, Dad, you've told us that story a million times," Zack insisted.

Bill didn't let Zack deter him. "My father bought this coin in 1962," he continued, staring at the penny. "He gave the watch and coin to me when I turned sixteen, just weeks before he died."

Zack sat up, hearing this part of the story for the first time. "Does that mean you're giving them to me next month when I turn sixteen?" he asked, walking over to his dad to take a better look at the coin. Zack stared at the watch as if he expected Bill to hand it and The Lincoln over to him right then and there.

"Uh," his father said. He paused, then added a definitive, "No."

Disappointed with his dad's answer, Zack reached out for The Lincoln, barely grazing the penny. *SNAP!* A spark shot out, scorching his finger, and he jerked his hand away. Everyone at the table saw Zack flinch as a bolt of electricity shot up his arm. His eyes widened and he let out a squeal.

Carly saw the strange look on Zack's face, and her hand flew to her mouth to try to keep her iced tea from spraying across the table. Her dad gave her *the eye*, and she swallowed hard, using her napkin to hide her smile.

"OUCH!" Zack yelled.

Bill quickly grabbed Zack's hand, examining the black mark left on Zack's finger. He glanced over at Sam, exchanging looks of concern.

"Are you okay?" Sharon asked.

"I can't feel my fingers," Zack replied with a twisted expression.

Carly made a snorting sound, trying as hard as she could not to burst out laughing.

"I'm serious, are you all right?" his mother repeated.

"Yeah, I'll be okay," he said, walking back to his chair shaking his arm.

You deserved to get shocked! Carly thought. Hate was a strong word, and Carly refused to waste that much energy on the likes of Zack Marshall. Serious dislike better described her feelings about his many annoying personality traits. She couldn't stand his constant need to be the center of attention, or the fact that he treated his little brother Kevin as if he didn't exist. Not to mention the disrespectful way he always spoke to his mother. Carly knew he'd never speak to his dad that way.

"I don't see what's so special about The Lincoln anyway," Zack spouted, flexing his fingers and sinking into his seat. "It's just a stupid penny."

"A stupid penny?" his father shot back. "You want me to tell you what's so special about The Lincoln?" Bill pushed his chair back and stood up, still holding the watch. "Do you really want to know?" he repeated, raising his voice. Bill's face turned beet red as he stared at Zack.

With a look of embarrassment at his dad's reaction, Zack didn't say a word, and with the sudden tension at the table, neither did anyone else. Sharon's eyes widened and she coughed. Carly saw Sam look at Bill with one eye squinted, and recognized the expression that he had just given her moments ago. She and her brother called it *the eye*. It was the look her dad used to say, "You'd better stop right now." *But*, Carly wondered, *why would Dad be giving Bill the eye?*

"Don't get your father all fired up over The Lincoln," Sam said, breaking the silence, "or we'll be here all night while he describes every single detail that makes that coin special."

Carly stared at the pocket watch Bill was holding, trying to make out the design carved into the cover. It looked like a flower, but before she could tell for sure, Bill closed the watch and returned it to his pocket.

"Listen to Sam, he knows what he's talking about," Bill said.

Sharon let out the breath she'd been holding, seeming relieved that Bill's rant had stopped. "Help me get this table cleared so we can bring out the cake," she told Kevin and Zack. "Carly, are you finished with your veggie burger?"

"Yes, thank you," Carly replied, grateful for having had a meatless option after coming to Bill's birthday dinner straight from gymnastics. She was no purest vegan by any stretch of the imagination, because that would mean giving up cheese, which was something she would never do. But to say she found the smell of meat unappetizing would be an understatement. Actually, she found it revolting, and never touched the stuff.

"Can I help?" Carly offered.

"No honey, the boys can do it," Sharon told her. Carly heard Zack mumble something, but tuned him out like she had been trying to do since the minute she got to his house.

Carly watched Sharon carry what was left of the baked beans and potato salad up the stone pathway to the house. She was dressed in her usual beige and white, and her shoulder-length blonde hair was styled perfectly. With never a hair out of place, Sharon looked pretty much the same every time you saw her. Carly remembered how much they relied on Sharon when her mom was sick, and looking across the table at her brother, she wondered if he was thinking the same thing.

Gracefully slipping out of her chair, Carly walked to the edge of the pool, admiring the huge shade trees that blocked the views of the neighboring homes, and the flower boxes overflowing with spring flowers. On the other side of the sparkling pool was a two-bedroom guesthouse with a wall of French doors reflecting the image of the main house. She frowned, feeling a pang of jealousy, remembering how beautiful her own backyard used to be. Now the shriveled sticks poking out of the dried dirt only screamed of her mother's absence.

"Did my girl lose her beautiful smile?" Carly thought she heard her mother's soothing voice ask. Her throat burned and she tried to swallow as she glanced over her shoulder, but there was no one there. It was just her mind playing tricks again. She knew that it couldn't have really been her mother's voice. That would've been impossible.

Carly noticed her dad looking at her as he and Bill droned on about their last round of golf. Sam and Bill were childhood friends, so it wasn't a stretch when they became business partners and opened their advertising firm, Romano and Marshall. Ever since her mother died last year, all her father did was work and play golf at the club. To tell the truth, he wasn't around much before she got sick, but during those last months he rarely left her mother's side. Carly, her father, and her older brother Ben were with her mother when she took her last breath. It was the toughest thing Carly had ever experienced, and she doubted she would ever get over it.

+++++++++

Zack

Zack, Sharon, and Kevin returned with a double chocolate cake, singing "Happy Birthday" as they walked. Kevin put the small plates he was carrying on the table next to the cake while Sharon sliced several pieces.

"I have a present for you," Sam said, sliding a plastic sleeve with a coin inside in front of Bill.

"I said no presents," Bill insisted as he took the coin out of the plastic. It was a 1943 steel penny. He laughed and winked at Sam.

"Aww man, not another coin." Zack reached for the cake Sharon was passing him. "Now we're going to have to hear about coins all night."

"Hey," Bill said to Zack. "Your grandfather introduced Sam and me to coin collecting when we were kids. It's too bad you guys aren't interested. People would kill for mine or Sam's collection that you call boring."

"Let me see what Sam gave you." Kevin leaned over and took the penny from his dad. "Wow, how cool!"

"You're such a suck-up," Zack whispered as he nudged Kevin's shoulder.

"Zack!" his mother reprimanded.

Kevin pinched the coin between his fingers, examining each side. "Its gray color makes it look like a nickel or a dime. But that's Abraham Lincoln, so it must be a penny." He handed the coin to Carly.

"Is it real? Can you spend it?" she asked before passing the coin across the table to Ben.

"Oh, it's real," Bill assured her.

"How much is this thing worth?" Ben asked, giving it to Zack.

"This one is in good shape, so from a collector's standpoint, it's worth about fifty cents," Sam said.

"Fifty cents? That's all? Why do you guys collect these stupid things if they're not worth anything?" Zack blurted as he got up and carried the coin back to his dad.

"Because the value of a coin isn't always determined by what someone will pay for it." A wry smile crept over his face. "I hope this penny brings you good luck in finding all the coins that you look for."

"Thanks, I have a feeling it will." Bill smiled.

"Can I have another piece of cake?" Kevin asked.

"Me too," Zack and Ben both chimed.

"Sure, hand me your plates," Sharon told the boys.

"Hey, Ben, your dad said that you have some big music producer wanting to see your band," Bill said.

"Yeah, his name is Kenny Martin. He owns the studio where our guitar player, Taylor, interned last summer. He's coming to see us play at the school dance in a couple weeks," Ben replied.

"That's great," Bill said.

"When you become rich and famous, don't forget who's been your number-one roadie," Zack said.

"And your number two," Kevin added.

Zack made a face, but he knew Kevin was right. He, his brother, and Carly had helped out at all of Ben's shows.

"I sat with Mrs. Parker at a luncheon last week and she mentioned that her son Adam is in your band," Sharon said.

"Yeah, Adam plays drums and Brandon Reed is our bass player."

"Do you guys have a name?" she asked.

"We haven't agreed on one yet."

"*Cut Wind* gets my vote." Zack chuckled, and everyone but Carly laughed.

"That gets my vote as well," Sam agreed. "How about you, Zack? When's your next game?"

"We've got a big one the day after we get back from Hawaii. Justin and I both got three hits off this pitcher the last time we faced him. We plan on doing it again!"

"Well, good luck!" Sam told him. "And Kevin, I guess you're the man! Coming in first place in that computer science competition is huge."

"Thanks! It was pretty awesome," Kevin replied.

"How does it feel to be a genius?"

"I'm not a genius," Kevin said, shifting in his chair.

Carly sat staring through the clump of dark hair hanging in her face at the ice swimming in her glass.

"Carly, what have you been up to?" Bill asked.

"Nothing, really," she mumbled.

"Now, that's not true. You're doing well at gymnastics," Sam offered.

Carly kept her eyes on the ice and didn't say a word. There was an awkward pause. Zack's eyebrows bunched together as he stared at her, shaking his head. *You're so weird!*

Bill and Sam turned the conversation to golf, and Zack thought he was going to die of boredom. He looked at the mark on his finger, and with his hand still numb, he jiggled it, trying to get the feeling back. "May we go back to the game house now?" he finally asked, interrupting his dad's seemingly endless story.

"Game house?" Sam asked.

"Yes, since we've had them move all their gaming devices out to the guesthouse, they've been calling it the game house," Sharon replied.

"Well, can we?" Zack asked impatiently.

"I don't think so. You've spent enough time playing video games for today," his mother told him. "You do have restricted gaming privileges, remember?"

"That's not fair!" Zack spouted.

"Zack," his father warned.

His mother straightened up in her chair. "Well, I don't think it's fair that I had to take a call from your math teacher because you didn't do your homework."

"But I did the homework. I just forgot it at home," Zack snapped.

"Funny how you seem to remember everything there is to know about baseball, but can't remember to turn in your homework," she added.

"You're not being fair!" Zack yelled as he stood up, pressing his lips together and glaring at his mother.

Bill stopped mid-sentence. "Zack!" he shouted.

Zack folded his arms and threw himself back onto the chair.

"We've got to be going," Sam said, getting to his feet. "We need to finish packing for tomorrow."

Carly jumped up like she had been shot from a cannon and was halfway to the gate before turning and saying goodbye.

"See you tomorrow," Ben said, nudging Zack as he got up.

"Yeah," Zack muttered as he sat sulking. He waited until his parents were seeing the Romanos to their car, then ran into the house, slamming the door to his room.

CHAPTER TWO

DRAWING A BLANK

Zack

L ater that night, Zack lay on his bed and closed his eyes. That's when the vision came. He could see himself approaching the classroom door. *STOP!* He pulled the covers over his head, but that didn't prevent his brain from betraying him. Halfway between sleep and waking, the memory came flooding back.

++++++++++

The butterflies in Zack's stomach were the size of bats when he stepped into the classroom at the precise moment the second bell rang.

"Cutting it rather close, aren't we, Mr. Marshall?" Mr. Baumgart sneered.

Mr. Baumgart had taught math at View Crest High School for as long as anyone could remember. Most teachers had their favorites, their "teacher's pets," but he took a different approach with his pupils. For some unknown reason Mr. Baumgart preferred to select students to dislike, and create problems for them while they were in his class. This year during first period, Zack was that student.

Zack made his way to the back of the room and collapsed into the seat next to Ben. "Just made it," Zack said over the noise in the classroom.

"You're crazy. You know he's after you," Ben said.

"Yeah." Zack pushed his backpack under his chair. "I stayed up way too late last night working on the stupid homework he gave us and couldn't wake up this morning. I wanted to make sure that I at least get some answers right this time."

"Quiet!" Mr. Baumgart called out in a high-pitched voice. The room was suddenly so silent you could have heard a pin drop. No one would risk being singled out. Mr. Baumgart addressed his class with authority, but it was apparent by his appearance that a classroom of high school students was the only place he could command such attention.

He wasn't much taller than the boys in his class. The clothes he wore were either too tight or too loose. The students referred to him as "Bum," which had more to do with the way he looked than his name. Today, he wore a short-sleeve shirt that had been white at one time, but was now a grayish color. While the shirt sagged at his shoulders, the buttons down the front struggled to stay closed over his bowling ball-shaped belly. With his shirt tucked in, he needed a cinched belt to hold his pants up. The hair remaining on his head was a peculiar shade of orange, which he parted just above the ear. Twenty or so long hairs were swept over the top of his head in an attempt to disguise his baldness. No one was fooled.

"Homework assignments out and pass them to the person in front of you," Mr. Baumgart directed. "I will give you the correct answers, and you will write the number of incorrect answers at the top of the page."

The sound of bags being unzipped and papers shuffling filled the room. Zack looked into his backpack.

"Oh no," he said quietly as he frantically rifled through the folders and books. "My worksheet isn't here." His mind's eye could see the paper sitting on the end of his bed where he left it, and he slumped forward. "All that work for nothing."

"Oh man, you're in for it," Ben told him.

Mr. Baumgart looked over at the girl in front of Zack with no paper to correct. A sinister smile crept onto his face as he strolled across the room, heading straight for Zack. Zack saw him coming and the bat-sized butterflies in his stomach began fighting for space.

"Mr. Marshall, did you think the assignment did not apply to you? You must have mistaken this class for one of your others that allows its school athletes to do whatever they please."

"I left my homework at home," Zack said with his eyes focused on the ground, not wanting to see Mr. Baumgart's reaction.

The teacher's laughter sounded like the bark of a seal. "Oh, that's original. Are you sure your dog didn't eat it?"

There was a stir in the room.

"Mr. Marshall, take out your book and turn to the page with yesterday's homework assignment." He walked back to the front of the class. "I want you to choose an equation to complete up here at the board." With his arms folded and a smirk on his face, he leaned back against the desk. "I'm sure we would all be delighted for you to enlighten us on how to correctly solve the problem."

This wasn't the first time the teacher had him work something out in front of the class, and the times before hadn't gone well, but Zack thought today would be different. He was prepared. He had studied all night, and there was a glimmer of hope that he could pull this off.

After copying the equation onto the blackboard, he stared at the numbers, unsure of where to begin. Off to the side he began writing random numbers, racking his brain for the formula he used on his homework the night before. The eyes of his fellow students bored into his back like lasers, which wasn't helping the situation. His mind went completely blank, and the harder he tried to remember, the more nothing came. He stood there in a silent panic, not knowing what to do next.

"If you completed your homework as you say you did, working this out should be easy for you," Mr. Baumgart announced. He moved closer to the blackboard, and in a quiet, scornful voice said, "I can't figure out if you're stupid or just lazy." Zack stood there with his eyes glued to the chalkboard, while Baumgart pushed harder. "You're a big shot out there on the baseball field, aren't you? Look at yourself," he said with disgust. "In here you're nothing."

Zack knew what Baumgart was trying to do, and he wasn't going to let himself get sucked into it this time. He'd learned early in the school year that defending himself only made Baumgart come down harder. He stared straight ahead, ignoring his teacher as he shifted from one foot to the other for what seemed like an eternity, until the bell finally rang and Ben handed him his backpack. They walked by Baumgart's desk as they left the classroom.

"Mr. Marshall, I will be contacting your parents," the smug voice said. "I'm sure they will be interested to know that you failed to turn in yet another homework assignment."

Zack pretended not to hear and kept walking.

The replay of what he'd experienced the previous Friday was over, and his blankets rose and fell as he was finally able to fall asleep.

CHAPTER THREE

THE ABDUCTION

Carly

The gymnastics instructor peeked her head in the doorway. "Carly, your dad is here."

Carly looked at her phone and saw that it was just before one o'clock. *He's early, and he's never early.* Dropping her phone down on the chair next to her, she rushed to unzip her bag. She threw her shorts and T-shirt on over her leotard, slipped her feet into her sneakers, and grabbing her bag, she hurried out the door. Bill was in the passenger seat of the Range Rover, so she opened the back door and climbed in.

"Hi sweetie, did you have fun?" her father asked.

"I guess," she replied, rolling her eyes at the ridiculous question as she snapped her seat belt. *Fun? Really? I'm only going here so you'll quit bugging me about getting back to normal.*

"Hello, Carly," Bill said.

"Hi," she replied, barely louder than a whisper. She stared out at the jagged mountains. Although it was only spring, the hillsides were already turning brown.

Sam pulled out of the parking lot and drove down the street to Topanga Canyon Boulevard. "I don't know why there's not a traffic light at this corner. It has to be one of the toughest left turns in Los Angeles," he remarked. The cars sped around the curves of the windy road as he waited for an opening. "Bill and I are going to the club to pick up our golf clubs for the trip. We'll probably play nine holes while we're there," he informed Carly. "You won't mind if I drop you off with Ben for a couple hours?"

Her head fell back against the headrest. *You're so sneaky. Why don't you just come right out and say, I'm taking you to Zack's house?*

"Or you could call your friend Torie. Maybe you two could do something together this afternoon," he added.

It's so obvious what you're trying to do. I haven't spoken to Torie since Mom's funeral, she thought. She looked at the back of her dad's head. *Why do you push me to act the way I did before? Why am I not good enough the way I am?*

She forced herself to speak. "No thanks, you can just take me home." She knew he would never agree to it, but thought it was worth a try.

"Sweetie, I don't want you sitting home alone," Sam replied. "I told Ben I would probably be bringing you by. It won't be for very long. Afterward, I'll meet you two at the house and we'll get some dinner before we go to the airport."

She took a deep breath. "Okay." There wasn't much she could say with Bill in the car. The last thing she wanted to do was spend the first day of spring break hanging out at the Marshalls', but it looked like she had no choice.

The traffic light that usually stayed red forever was green when they approached, forcing them to arrive at the Marshalls' much too quickly as far as Carly was concerned. She opened the door and, taking her bag, she stepped out, slamming the door behind her.

Sharon came down the driveway and Bill rolled down his window. "Everything is packed and ready to go. I just need to run up to the mall before I start dinner," she said.

"That's fine," Bill replied. "We'll be home after we get in nine holes."

"Okay. I thought we'd eat around five o'clock. The car to the airport will be here at eight." Sharon leaned closer to the window. "Sam, we'll pick you and the kids up right after that. Don't cut it too close. I don't want to start this trip running late. You know how traffic can be."

"I'll make sure he gets home on time," Sam replied.

Sharon laughed. "That's great coming from the one who's never on time."

Sam smiled and shrugged his shoulders. He looked at Carly standing in the driveway. "Sweetie, you and Ben meet me at the house at four o'clock. I'll let you choose the restaurant," he said, as if it were some consolation.

Big deal! Even with her hair half in her face, she knew her dad could see exactly how she felt about being at the Marshalls'. Without saying a word, she turned and walked around the side of the house, passing three bikes that were leaning against the wall. She opened the wooden gate and entered the backyard. After only a few steps, she heard the familiar shouts from the boys in the guesthouse. *How can they play those stupid games every single day? What a useless waste of time.* She entered the open guesthouse door and saw Ben and Zack on the couch with Kevin in the chair next to them. They were all staring at the screen.

Ben's head bobbed up at the sound of her bag hitting the floor. "Hey, Sis."

There was a loud explosion on the screen, and Zack's fists flew up in the air.

"We have a new champion," Zack announced, strutting around the room.

Ben fell back on the couch as if he were dead. Carly shook her head in disgust and sat down on the leather chair nearest the door. She closed her eyes as she leaned back, wishing she were anywhere but here.

"My turn," Kevin said, already reaching for the controller.

Ben stood up to trade places with him.

"This won't take long, so don't go anywhere," Zack told Ben as he walked over to the fridge and grabbed a soda.

Sharon appeared in the doorway with her purse and keys in hand. "I'm running to the mall, and while I'm gone, I want you to go get your sports bag from Ben's house so that I can wash your baseball uniform before we leave tonight," she told Zack.

"You need it right now?" Zack complained. "I can't stop playing now, I'm on a roll."

"You never listen," his mother told him. "I asked you to have it here by the time I get back."

"Okay, okay. I'll get it," he said, waving her out of the room so he and Kevin could get started.

"Pick your battles," Carly heard Sharon say under her breath as she left the guesthouse.

Carly looked at Ben, who was hunkered down in the oversized leather chair, staring at the screen. "Dad said to meet him at the house at four o'clock."

"What time is it now?" Ben asked.

She felt her pocket for her phone and stopped. It wasn't there. In a panic, she began rummaging through her bag.

"Crap!" Her outburst startled Zack, causing him to lose focus.

"Hey," he shouted as he lost a point to Kevin.

"What's the matter?" Ben asked, watching her frantically search her bag.

"My phone," Carly said, remembering she had put it down next to her while she was changing. "I left my phone at gymnastics."

"Call Dad and ask him to pick it up on his way back," Ben told her.

"You know he turns his phone off when he's on the course," she said, letting go of her bag.

"Here, just try calling him." Ben tossed her his phone.

Carly pressed Ben's code to open the screen and saw there were two missed calls from his ex-girlfriend, Francesca. *Maybe she's not going to be an "ex" for long.* A fleeting smile crossed her face. She called her dad's number, hanging up when it went straight to voice mail.

"Crap!" she said again.

"We can go by and get it when Dad picks us up for dinner," Ben offered.

"No, we can't. They close at three today," Carly replied.

"Well then, I don't know what to tell you." Ben shrugged.

"I've got to go get it!" she insisted.

"Not by yourself, you're not."

"Okay then, come with me. We'll take our bikes and use the shortcut," she said, eager at the thought.

"That path will only take us halfway. We'll get killed trying to get the rest of the way up Topanga. Why don't you just call your instructor and have her hide your phone somewhere outside, then when Dad comes home he can take you to get it." Ben got up and started walking down the hall.

"I can't take the chance of something happening to it. We leave tonight and I'm not going anywhere for five days without my phone," she called to him as she heard the bathroom door close.

"Hey, take it," Zack yelled, but before he could say "outside," there was an explosion on the screen and Zack's man was down. Kevin's hands flew up in the air.

"I finally beat my brother." Kevin sang the words, skipping around the room.

Zack turned to Carly. "What is your problem? Don't you see we've got something important going on here? Go spew your nonsense somewhere else." He glared at Kevin, then back at Carly. "What do you need your phone for anyway?" he said, lowering his voice to barely a whisper. "It's not like anyone is going to call you. Who would want to talk to the little freak that walks around bummed out all the time?" He pointed at Kevin. "You have less friends than egghead here," he laughed.

"Shut up!" Kevin snapped, no longer celebrating his win. "Shut up, now!"

Carly slowly stood up with her eyes locked on Zack. If looks could kill, he would have dropped dead right there. "You're such a giant cretin!" she fumed.

Before he could speak another word, she grabbed her bag and stormed out of the guesthouse, slamming the door so hard that the windows rattled. Every inch of her body trembled as she threw open the gate. *What a jerk!* She grabbed Ben's bike that was leaning against the garage. Quickly wrapping the handles of her bag around the handlebars, she jumped on and sped down the street.

It was official. Her feelings toward Zack had definitely been upgraded to hate. Her eyes began to well up. *I'm not going to cry over something that idiot said,* she told herself as tears fell from her cheeks. *I used to have plenty of friends. More friends than he'll ever have.* She pedaled so fast that she blew through the four-way stop at the corner. *I don't care what Ben says, I'm going to get my phone.*

Turning at the cul-de-sac, she rode up the curb to the wooded path leading to Topanga Canyon Boulevard. Huge rocks made the pathway anything but straight, and with an occasional stump left by a fallen tree, the ride became a struggle to stay upright. But she didn't care. She was still reeling from Zack's words. *"The freak that walks around bummed out."* *If he only knew what it was like to lose your mother, he would know that "bummed out" didn't cover the half of it.*

With one foot on the pedal and the other on the ground, she breathed heavily as she slowly plodded her way up the hill. A large branch lying across the path forced her to get off and maneuver around to the front of the bike. *What am I supposed to do, be a big fake? Laugh and act all cheery? That would sure make my dad happy.* She yanked her front tire over the branch. *Everyone expects me to go on as if things are normal. Look around, people! Everything is NOT normal! My mom is GONE!*

Holding the handlebars, she pulled the bike as hard as she could until the back tire cleared the portion of the fallen tree branch blocking her way. No longer able to hold her emotions in check, she bent forward, and her shoulders shook as her tears hit the ground. *Mom, I miss you so much. Please help me. I've lost my smile*, she thought burying her face in her arm. Her body convulsed as she tried to catch her breath. *But that doesn't make me a freak! Zack is such a loser!* She wiped her face on the sleeve of her T-shirt. *He would never have said those things if Ben had been in the room.*

She threw her leg over the bike and continued making her way up the hill until the path dead-ended onto a clearing next to a busy two-lane street. Immediately, she could see that Ben was right. Only someone with a death wish would try to make it up Topanga Canyon Boulevard on bike. As she watched the passing flow of speeding cars, she tried to dig deep for the courage to ride beside them. *After all, I made it this far.* In the openings between the cars that flew past, she saw a Range Rover pulling into the parking lot of the lookout across the street and recognized the bike rack on the back. *That's Dad's car. Perfect timing for once. Ben must have told him I was up here.*

She caught sight of a black car with darkened windows also entering the parking lot, followed by a white van that stopped directly behind the Range Rover. Between the passing cars, she was able to catch glimpses of her dad and Bill, who were now out of the car, speaking with two men from the van. She couldn't see their faces, but one of the men was very tall and the other was half his size.

"DAAAD!" she cried, letting the bike fall to the ground as she jumped up and down trying to get his attention. Her voice was drowned out by the traffic, and he didn't seem to notice she was there. *Why isn't he looking for me?* She stood waving her arms. *He's here to pick me up, isn't he?*

While waiting for a chance to cross, she watched the four men, who appeared to be arguing. *What's going on over there?* Determined to get across, she looked up and down the street, but there was no break in the steady stream of cars. Her eyes went back to her dad. He was walking back toward the Range Rover, but before he reached the door, the smaller of the two men ran after him and shoved him to the ground. She watched the man and her father struggle as Bill rushed over to help Sam.

"DAAAD!" she screamed. A slow-moving semi-truck came between her and the lookout, blocking her view. Anxious to know what was happening, she rushed to the curb and knelt down, looking underneath the semi, but couldn't see a thing. Finally, the truck passed and she had a clear view. Her stomach lurched and she froze. The tall man had a gun and was herding her dad and Bill into the back of the van. Terrified by what she was witnessing, she quickly looked up and down the street, but there was no way she could cross.

She shifted her focus back to the van. The doors were closed and Bill and Sam were nowhere in sight. Suddenly, a cloud of dust was being kicked up behind the van as it came barreling out into traffic, nearly colliding with another car.

"NOOO!" Carly screamed, stepping into the street. Her eyes widened as she watched the van disappear around the bend with her dad and Bill inside. "COME BAAACK!"

The blast from the horn of the car swerving around her jolted her back into the moment, and she returned to the clearing. *Oh my God! Where are they going? I have to call the police!* Looking up the mountain road, she knew she would never make it to her phone; it was stupid of her to think she could. The fastest way to get help was to take the path back down. She stood the bike up and glanced back at the lookout across the street. The Range Rover sat with the doors open, and although she hadn't seen it leave, the black car was gone.

Without wasting another second, she spun the bike around and started down the path. It was a steep descent, and she could tell she was going to get down much faster than she had gotten up. Even riding the brake didn't slow her down as her tires slid forward on leaves and pebbles covering the ground. She locked her elbows, trying to keep the bike straight as she picked up speed, but the rough terrain grabbed her front wheel, jerking it back and forth. Out of control, she was rapidly approaching the tree limb that had blocked the trail on the way up. *That stupid branch!* With her foot pressing down on the brake as hard as she could, she leaned to her side, trying to slow down. A rock snagged her foot, sending the front of the bike plowing into the tree branch and catapulting her into a huge boulder. Her limp body slid to the ground.

Dazed, she opened her eyes and pushed her hair out of her face. Unaware of how long she had been lying there, she was afraid to move, terrified at how badly she may be injured. She slowly got to her feet, and a stabbing pain shot through her leg. She noticed a trickle of blood running from her cut knee. The pain was excruciating, but she could move and that was all that mattered. *I have to get down the hill.* She looked to the sky. "Mom, please help me!"

Unable to put her full weight on her left leg, she hobbled back to the bike. The handlebars were turned backward and the front tire was flat. "Great!" She looked around for her bag but didn't see it, grabbing the seat and handlebars, she dragged the bike over the tree branch. The image of the van speeding off with Bill and her dad ran through her mind. She quickly stood the bike up and limped along next to it, making her way down the hill as fast as she could.

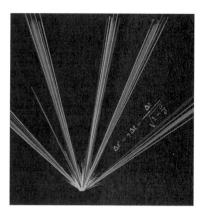

CHAPTER FOUR

THE BLUE BEAM

Zack

A glowing white light filled the television screen, followed by the sound of an explosion. Zack's arms flew up, and Ben fell onto the couch. Kevin's head dropped, obviously disappointed that his brother had just chalked up another win. Zack could hear his mother approaching the guesthouse and knew he was in trouble before she even walked through the door.

"Where's your baseball uniform?" she asked.

"Umm, I didn't exactly go get it yet," he replied.

"There's no *exactly*." Her voice became shrill. "Either you did what I asked or you didn't."

"Mom, I tried, but there were these aliens and they tried to take Kevin, so I—"

Sharon stopped him from going any further. "Why do you always make up ridiculous stories when I ask you something?" she questioned.

Zack just snickered.

"You should know that I'm not doing laundry the night we get home, so if you want to wear a smelly baseball uniform that's been sitting in a bag for a week to your game on Sunday, that's fine with me," she stated before turning and walking out of the guesthouse.

"Okay, okay! Don't have a meltdown. I'll go get it," he called after her, rolling his eyes.

Zack shook his head, taken aback that his mother would speak to him that way in front of his friend, even if it was just Ben. It only added more support to his theory that when a child is born, parents were given a huge needle so that they could burst their kid's bubble at will, and his mother used the one she was given on a regular basis.

"Come on," he said to Ben.

Ben looked at his phone and saw that it was four o'clock. "Yeah, I've got to get home."

They left the guesthouse and went through the side gate.

"Carly must have taken my bike," Ben said, pointing at the two bikes leaning against the garage. He looked at Zack. "Man, I wish you two would stop going at each other."

Zack ignored Ben's comment as he watched Kevin mount one of the bikes. "You've got to be kidding me. Do you have to follow me everywhere?" he asked. "I'm just going down the street."

Kevin made a face at his brother and circled around, riding slowly behind Ben and Zack as they walked.

"You know, I just don't get her," Zack said, still abashed over his mother's behavior. "She makes a huge deal out of everything. If things aren't exactly the way she wants them, she freaks out."

They stopped and waited for a car to turn at the four-way stop before continuing to the next corner. Kevin rode down the curb into the street and noticed someone moving at the end of the cul-de-sac.

"Look! There's Carly!" he yelled, taking off toward her with Ben and Zack following.

+++++++++

Carly

Carly hobbled next to Ben's bike. Her T-shirt was ripped and blotched with dirt. Leaves were stuck in her hair, and a thin trail of dried blood ran down her leg.

"Sis, what happened? You're a wreck!" Ben exclaimed, taking the bike from her and letting it fall as he held her arm for support.

"Thank God you're here!" Carly said. "Dad and Bill have been kidnapped. Give me your phone. I have to call the police." She held out her trembling hand, waiting for Ben to pass her his phone.

"What?" Zack asked.

"Kidnapped?" Kevin stared at her in confusion.

"What are you talking about? Look at you, you can barely walk," Ben said, observing the condition of her leg. "What happened?"

"It's not me, it's Dad. Just give me your phone!" she screamed.

"Okay, here." Ben handed her his phone. She pushed 911 and, holding the phone to her ear, she filled the boys in as fast as she could.

"I went up the path to Topanga," she began.

"I told you not to do that," Ben said.

"Shut up and listen," she told him, still waiting for her 911 call to go through. "I got to the top and saw Dad's car at the lookout."

"What would he be doing up there?" Ben questioned.

"You didn't send him to pick me up?"

"No," he replied.

Silent for only a second, she waved her hand as if to brush away her thoughts. "That doesn't matter," she continued. "There were two men, and they had a gun. Something was wrong, because they were arguing. The next thing I knew, one of them had Dad on the ground."

"What?" Ben yelled.

"I swear," she said, practically in tears. "It was awful. They forced Dad and Bill into their van and took off." She realized that her call was not connecting and looked at the screen. "Nothing is happening," she cried, handing Ben his phone.

Ben examined the phone. "There's no reception. Give me yours," he said to Zack.

"I think you've lost your mind." Zack reached into his pocket and handed Ben his phone.

"I'm not crazy! I saw it with my own eyes!" Carly shouted.

"Where did the van go?" Kevin asked.

"Down Topanga," Carly replied.

"This phone isn't getting reception either," Ben said.

"We need to get to a phone that works!" Carly stated.

A breeze kicked up, carrying an unusual chill, and Zack shivered.

"Get on," Kevin told her, gesturing at his bike seat.

Ben quickly grabbed the handlebars of the bike on the ground and stood it up, preparing to run home.

A cold wind blew and Carly hunched her shoulders, folding her arms around herself. "What's going on out here? It's freezing." She started toward Kevin's bike, but stopped. "Wait," she whispered, pushing her hair out of her face. Her eyebrows furrowed.

Zack and Ben didn't move.

There was an eeriness about the way she slowly looked around. "Do you feel that?" she asked, seeing her breath in the cold air as she spoke.

"Feel what?" Kevin stared at her frightened face. "What is it? You're creeping me out!"

Carly didn't answer. There was electricity in the air that she couldn't find the words to describe. The sound of rustling leaves drew her attention, and her head jerked around, fixating on the trail. "There's someone there," she cautioned. The hairs on her arms stood up and a prickly sensation ran down her spine. She braced herself to run.

"Hurry and get on," Kevin pleaded, poised to take off as soon as she was on the back of his bike. But her eyes didn't move from the trail.

"There's no one there," Ben assured her.

"I've got a bad feeling," Carly warned.

Before she could take a step toward Kevin, a powerful gust of wind came whistling through the trail. The leaves and small rocks that had made Carly's ride so difficult had been picked up and were swirling toward them. They turned their backs and ducked under their arms, but couldn't avoid being pelted with all that the wind was carrying. The strong force blew them back a few steps, and they struggled to remain standing. Kevin fell to the ground and watched his bike slide down the street. After a few seconds, the wind abruptly stopped.

It hadn't lasted very long, but it was so intense that it left them stunned and covered with dirt. Carly glanced back at the trail, wiping her face with the inside of her shirt.

"What the heck was that?" Ben brushed himself off, moving closer to Carly.

"Geez," Zack said, spitting the grime from his mouth.

Kevin made his way over to his bike. His legs looked rubbery as he walked, and he seemed disoriented.

"Are you okay, Kevin?" Ben called to him.

Kevin didn't answer as he picked up his bike and zigzagged back toward them, steering straight into Zack.

Zack jumped back. "Watch what you're doing, dork."

"Sorry, I didn't mean to," Kevin apologized, backing away.

Zack bent down to rub the scratch on his leg left by Kevin's wheel and heard something. He put his finger to his lips. "Shh, listen. Do you hear that?"

Kevin got off of his bike, and they all crouched down with their heads cocked. The sound seemed to be coming from the ground. Ben closed his eyes, straining to hear the slight buzzing noise like a ringing in his ears. Movement drew their attention to the middle of the street as a glint of sunlight reflected off a shiny coin that was rolling toward them.

+++++++++

Zack

Before it reached them, the coin fell over, and the sound of metal teetering from side to side filled the air. They stood staring at the small spot on the ground as it began to glow. Zack felt drawn to it and moved closer. With a flash, the glow became a bright light. Kevin tried to get over to Zack, but a powerful force rooted them all in place. Even though Ben was standing between Carly and the coin, he couldn't shield her from its effects. Unable to move their legs they cried out with their arms flailing as they fought to free themselves, but it was useless.

"What's that?" Kevin screamed, pointing to an iridescent purple line forming on the ground, circling around them and the coin.

Waves of heat hovered above the line on the pavement as it began churning. No one made a sound when a thin film sprung from it, forming walls around them that met above their heads, separating them from the outside world. Silence was replaced by a piercing high-pitched sound.

"What's happening?" Kevin cried, trying to shield his eyes from the bright light flooding the enclosure. Before anyone could answer, there was a jolt, and it felt as though they were being lifted.

"Are we moving?" Ben yelled.

"It sure feels like it," Zack said.

Suddenly, the bright light and the stabbing sound in their ears were gone, leaving them surrounded by an inky darkness. Terrified, they began screaming, only to become silent when they saw colored beams of light slowly growing out from the coin. The flowing movements of the red, yellow, and green shafts of light mesmerized Carly, Ben, and Kevin. A blue beam, not unlike a laser, shot out in Zack's direction and remained still. It was the only light not moving.

Zack could not take his eyes off of the blue beam. Floating above it were numbers and symbols that were being directed toward him. He could see the numbers forming mathematical equations in midair, then rearranging themselves into the answers to the problems. The movement was graceful yet deliberate, and Zack was hypnotized by what he was seeing.

Without words, he felt the blue beam reveal to him something much larger than the numbers it presented. "Yes, yes," was all he could say while nodding his head. Feeling no resistance or fear, he was overcome by a peacefulness unlike anything he'd ever experienced. The blue light showed him the simplicity of the complex problems it presented.

As quickly as they had been lifted, they were unexpectedly dropped to the ground. The dome dissipated, and they were released from the power that held them. It was over. Zack looked for the blue light, but it too was gone.

"What the heck just happened?" Ben said, anxiously turning to Carly. "Are you all right?"

"Yeah, just freaked out!" She squinted in the bright sunlight. "What was that thing?"

"I don't know, but let's get out of here before it happens again," Kevin remarked.

"I thought it was going to take us somewhere," Ben said.

"I thought so, too," Zack agreed, feeling the warmth of the sun.

They got to their feet and gathered around the coin, amazed to see that the source of what they had just experienced was a penny. Horns blaring the "Imperial March" came from Zack's phone, and they all flinched. The doomed *Star Wars* music was informing Zack he had a text from his mother. Looking at the phone, he could see there were several missed calls and a text saying it was urgent that they come home. He then noticed the time.

"It's almost five thirty; we've been gone for more than an hour," he announced.

"This is crazy!" Carly said. "We'll have to call the police from your house."

Zack ignored his phone when it sounded again and cautiously reached for the coin.

"Don't touch it," Kevin yelled. "Something bad might happen."

"Yeah, don't get any closer to it," Ben warned.

"I'm not just going to leave it here in the street," Zack declared, strangely not sharing their fear.

The others exchanged concerned glances while Zack touched the penny. Nothing happened. Carly and Kevin took a step back as Zack slowly picked up the coin.

"See," Zack said, turning it over in his hand and holding it out to Kevin. It appeared to be an ordinary penny. Zack's phone rang for the third time, and he put the coin in his pocket. "Let's go!"

CHAPTER FIVE

THE DISCOVERY

Carly

They rushed into the dining room to see a police officer standing next to Sharon with a notebook in his hand. Carly removed her arm from Ben's grasp, who had insisted on helping her, even though she had all but forgotten about her injured leg. She noticed a second officer standing off to the side. *They must have bad news.*

"Did you find our dads?" she asked desperately, slightly limping over to the chair that Kevin pulled out for her.

"Carly, what happened to you?" Sharon said, hurrying over to take a look at Carly's knee.

"I fell," Carly said, stretching out her leg.

"This is Carly and Ben Romano. It's their father's Range Rover that you found, and these are my sons Zack and Kevin," Sharon told the officers as she went for the first-aid kit in the cabinet.

"You asked if we found your fathers. How did you know they were missing?" the officer questioned.

"I was up on Topanga, across the street from the lookout," Carly replied, jerking her knee away as Sharon cleaned her wound. "I saw two men with a gun force my dad and Bill into a white van, then drive away."

Sharon gasped, dropping the tube of ointment. "Force them? With a gun? Were they hurt?"

"No, I don't think so," Carly replied.

Sharon's voice became louder. "Did you recognize the men?" she asked.

"No, I've never seen them before."

"Why didn't you call for help?" Sharon practically screamed.

"I tried to get to them, but there was too much traffic, and I had left my phone at gymnastics." Tears welled up in Carly's eyes.

"Mrs. Marshall, if you could, please calm down," the officer said. "We'll ask the questions from here." The officer paused before turning to Carly. "Did you get the license plate number of the van?"

"I couldn't see the plates," Carly replied, trying to regain her composure after Sharon's hysterical questioning.

"What did the men look like?"

"I couldn't see that either, but one of them was very tall, I mean super tall, and the other one barely came up to his waist. The small guy is the one who pushed my dad to the ground."

"What time did this happen?"

"It must have been around three o'clock," she guessed, trying to figure out the timeline. "I didn't have my phone, so I hurried back down the path to get help. These guys were there when I came off the trail." She gestured to the boys.

The officer looked at Zack. "How did you know she would be there?"

"We didn't," Zack replied. "We were on our way to their house when we saw her."

Sharon looked at the clock. "You left to go to Ben's at four o'clock. Where have you been for the last hour?"

"When we found Carly, we started to take her home, but all of a sudden it got really cold, so cold you could see your breath. Then a wind came out of nowhere," Zack began.

Sharon put her hand up for Zack to stop. "I don't want to hear another one of your stories," she warned.

"But Mom, it's not a story."

"Zack Marshall, knock it off!" Sharon yelled, losing her temper.

He was shocked by her outburst, but continued trying to explain. "Mom, this really did happen."

"He's telling the truth, Mom," Kevin butted in.

"Not you too?" she said. "I don't want to hear another word from either one of you," she added, pointing at each of them. "I'm sorry, Officer," she apologized. "We've had an issue with storytelling lately."

"I completely understand," the officer replied. "I'm going through the same thing with my daughter. We like to say she has a good imagination."

Zack stood there, staring a hole through his mother. Carly could practically see the steam coming out of his ears. She looked at Ben, and they silently agreed not to say anything about what they saw in the street.

"How did you know to come here?" Carly asked the officer.

The policeman who was observing them from the corner came forward. "We responded to a report of an abandoned Range Rover at a lookout on Topanga Canyon Boulevard. The driver and passenger doors were open with the motor running. The cell phones in the vehicle are what led us here," the officer explained. "Your account of what you witnessed is the first we are hearing of an abduction." He turned to Ben. "In light of this information, we'd like to take a look around your house. Have you contacted your mother?" he asked.

Sharon, having regained her composure, replied for him. "Their mother passed away."

"I'm sorry," the officer said, bowing slightly in Ben and Carly's direction. "Do you have family that live nearby?"

"My husband and I have legal guardianship if anything should happen to their father. They will be staying here with us until Bill and Sam get home," Sharon stated.

"That's probably for the best. The Department of Children and Family Services will be contacting you to see to the paperwork," the officer told her as he wrote in his notebook.

"My sister and I will need to get some things if we're going to stay here," Ben said. "I can show you the house. It's only a few blocks from here."

"That would be fine," the officer replied. "Has your father ever expressed to you that he was in any kind of trouble, or do you know of anyone that would want to harm him?"

"No, sir," Ben said.

Carly put her hands over her face. "Harm him?" Her mind kept replaying the gun being pointed at her dad. "We have to do something," she insisted.

Ben moved closer to Carly and put his hand on her shoulder.

"We will do everything possible to find your fathers," the officer said. "Gathering information is the first step in the process. We need to speak with Mrs. Marshall in private. When we're finished here, Officer McMurry and I will drive you to your house and see that you return safely, if Mrs. Marshall will allow it."

Still irritated with his mother, Zack looked at her. "Kevin and I are going with them," he said.

She nodded, and the four of them went out the front door to wait in the driveway.

"What's going on?" Carly said. "None of this makes sense."

"No, it doesn't," Kevin agreed.

"I can't believe my mom acted like that when I tried to tell her what happened when we found the coin," Zack said. "What? Did she think I was going to sit there and lie to the police?"

"You have heard of the boy who cried wolf, haven't you?" Carly asked.

Zack gave her a dirty look and walked back to the porch, sitting down on the step.

"Why would someone kidnap them?" he said, changing the subject.

"What were they doing in Topanga Canyon anyway?" Kevin joined Zack on the steps. "There are too many questions and no answers."

Ben folded his hands behind his back, leaning against the house, while Carly paced back and forth in front of him. Zack took the coin from his pocket and examined it. Carly stopped in her tracks when she saw the alarmed look on his face.

"What year were those twelve copper pennies pressed by mistake?" Zack asked.

"1943." Kevin and Carly both answered at the same time.

"I think we have a big problem," Zack said slowly, still staring at the coin.

"Another one? How could things get any worse?" Carly wanted to know.

"This penny." He paused as he turned it over again to analyze the other side. "I think this penny is The Lincoln," Zack answered.

"How can you be sure?" Ben asked.

"You heard my dad yesterday. The 1943 copper penny is one of the rarest coins in the world. So, what are the odds of my family having two of them?"

He extended his arm with the coin in the palm of his hand. The others gathered around to take a look for themselves. This was their first opportunity to see the coin up close since they'd found it in the street. The date on the coin struck fear in all of them.

"Where did the coin come from?" Carly asked.

"Obviously, from inside my dad's pocket watch," Zack snapped.

"I know that much. I mean how did it come to us?"

"How am I supposed to know?" Zack answered. "But from what we've seen so far, The Lincoln is no ordinary penny."

"They must be in serious trouble for your dad to let go of his coin," Ben said.

"Are we going to tell the police about finding the coin?" Kevin asked.

"Do you think they would believe us?" Zack replied.

"Probably about as much as your mom did," Carly said. "And if they do believe us, they'll definitely take the coin."

"Guaranteed, that's not going to happen," Zack said. "So, I guess we'd better keep it between ourselves."

"Okay," Kevin agreed. "I'm not really sure what happened anyway."

Ben saw Zack return the coin to his pocket. "Man, you're brave," he commented. "I wouldn't keep that thing in my pocket. What if it goes off again?"

Zack thought about it for a moment, then transferred the coin from his front to his back pocket and shrugged his shoulders. "Just in case."

++++++++++

The officers came out of the house and opened the back door to the police car for Ben, Carly, Zack, and Kevin to climb in. They pulled up in front of the Romanos', and one of the officers took Ben's house key, instructing them to stay in the police car while they searched the premises. It wasn't long before both officers returned, reporting that everything appeared to be in order and giving the four of them clearance to enter the house, while the officers waited in the car.

Once in the house, Carly grabbed some sweats and put them on top of her suitcase that was sitting packed and waiting to be taken on vacation. She followed Ben to the office to check on the safe; nothing appeared to be disturbed. Ben went to his room and came out with his backpack and guitar before heading to his father's room. The others walked in to find him sitting on the floor.

"What are you doing?" Zack asked.

"Give me a minute. Just let me find it," Ben told him as he ran his hand over the wood planks. "Here it is." He fingered the loose floorboard he was looking for and pulled it up, revealing a hollowed-out space.

"I never knew that was there," Carly said.

They all moved closer to see what was inside. Ben pulled out stacks of maps and a journal, stuffing them into his backpack. He looked into the hole to make sure he had removed everything and saw an old key lying in the corner.

"Hmm, I wonder what this key goes to," Ben said as he examined it. He replaced the piece of flooring and turned to Carly. "When dad showed me this hiding place, he told me that if anything should ever happen to him, we might need the things inside."

"What did you take out of there?" she asked.

"I have no idea."

CHAPTER SIX

AUNT TINA

Zack

The police car pulled up in front of the Marshalls' house, parking in the space that had just been vacated by a limousine. Zack checked the time on his phone. It had only been two hours since they'd found the coin, but it seemed like a lifetime.

"There goes Hawaii." Zack motioned in the direction of the limo that was now at the end of the block.

One of the officers assisted Ben and Carly in getting their bags from the trunk of the police car. "We'll be in contact," the officer informed them.

"Hey, isn't that Aunt Tina's car?" Kevin said as they passed the convertible parked in the driveway.

"How did she get here so fast?" Zack questioned, opening the front door.

A teary-eyed Aunt Tina rushed to greet them, hugging each one a bit too long. Zack was unsure if she was trying to console them or herself.

"Look at how big you've gotten." She backed away, examining both Zack and Ben. "The two of you must've grown a foot just since Christmas. You're taller than me!"

Zack raised his eyebrows and looked at Ben.

"Where's Uncle Eddie?" Zack asked.

"He's still in Fresno." Aunt Tina pulled a tissue from her pocket and wiped her eyes. "I was in Bakersfield when your mother called, so I came straight from there."

Sharon joined them in the entryway. "Zack, take Carly's bag upstairs, and get some of your things. You and Ben will be sleeping in the guesthouse."

Zack picked up Carly's heavy suitcase. The handle slipped out of his hand and the bag hit the floor with a thud. "What do you have in here, rocks?" he snarled.

"If it's too heavy for you, I can carry it myself," Carly snapped back.

Zack grunted as he labored up the stairs, more from the irritation of having to carry her bag than the actual weight of it. He put the suitcase down just inside the door of the guest room and it toppled over. *Let her deal with it.* He put his foot on the bag and pushed it further into the room before continuing to his room.

The globe on his desk immediately drew his attention. He stood there for a moment staring at planet Earth, feeling an odd connection to it. The blue beam came to mind, and the numbers it carried to him. His gaze moved to his laptop sitting next to the globe, which contained math assignments from his teacher, Mr. Baumgart. The sight of it usually produced angst, but now it stirred the type of rush he typically only experienced on the baseball field. He stared at his computer, confused by what he was feeling. *Weird!*

Once again, he thought of the blue light and tried to recall what it had communicated to him. *It seemed so important. But how could it mean anything? It was just a bunch of numbers.* He saw the blue light in his mind. *What were you trying to tell me?* He took in a deep breath and waited. Fragments of information floated in and out of his head, but none of it made any sense. Finally giving up, he grabbed his pillow and one of the baseball bats leaning against the wall and ran back downstairs.

"Where are your clothes?" Sharon asked.

"What clothes?" Zack replied, baffled by the question.

"I asked you to get your things to take out to the guesthouse."

"I did," he said, holding up his pillow and his bat.

Sharon closed her eyes and shook her head.

"Come on," Zack said, leading Ben out of the French doors.

"There are some inner tubes in the garage if you want to fix the tire on your bike," Zack told him as they entered the guesthouse.

"Cool, thanks," Ben replied.

Zack threw his pillow on the bed in one of the bedrooms. He opened the door to the other room. "You can sleep in here."

Ben put his guitar down and carried his backpack into the living room. He sat down in the big leather chair across from Zack, who was clearing the remote controls off the coffee table. Ben emptied his backpack of the things he had removed from under the floorboard, flipping through the notebook.

"What's all of this supposed to mean?" he asked, seeing pages with rows of random letters and numbers.

Zack wasn't paying any attention. He had been waiting for an opportunity to talk to Ben alone, and this was it. "When all that crazy stuff happened in the street, what did you see?" he asked, carefully unfolding one of the maps and laying it out on the table.

"A laser show cooler than anything I've ever seen before," Ben replied. "Why? Isn't that what you saw?"

"And then some." Zack took a deep breath, wondering if Ben was going to believe what he was about to tell him. "It was like the blue beam was telling me something."

"Really? Like what?"

Zack stared at the floor, trying to figure out how to explain what he saw but Carly and Kevin came rushing into the room before he could put it into words. They sat down on the couch with their eyes on the stacks of maps and the journal in front of them. Zack grabbed the journal and started paging through it.

"Have you figured out why Dad said we needed these things?" Carly asked.

"No," Ben said. "The journal is written in some kind of code."

"I can't make heads or tails of this stuff," Zack said. "The only writing that makes sense is this." He turned the journal around to show Carly and Kevin.

"TRUST NO ONE," were the only words on the page.

"That doesn't sound good," Carly said. "What's that on the cover?"

Zack closed the journal and saw the worn design on the front that he hadn't noticed—swirly rings with a design in the middle that he couldn't make out. He stared at the image, feeling as though he should know what the insignia meant, but he couldn't put his finger on it. "I don't know."

"Isn't that the same thing that was on the cover of your dad's pocket watch?" Carly asked as she looked closer.

"Let me see." Kevin took the book from Zack and examined the embossed symbol that was so old and faded it was hard to see. "Yeah, I think it is. It looks like an atom with an hourglass as its nucleus," he said.

"You're right! That's exactly what it is," Zack said.

"Wait," Ben said, pulling the key from his pocket and showing the others the twisted metal at its end. "The same design."

"It's cool looking," Carly added as Ben turned the key in his hand. "It must stand for something."

"Like what?" Zack asked.

"No idea," Carly said as she and Kevin moved down to the floor to get a better view of the maps.

"There's a total of twenty-one maps," Ben said, having laid out only a few of them on the table. Some were worn and faded, while others appeared to be brand new. None that they had unfolded showed any marks or handwriting.

"Are they all different locations?" Kevin asked, looking through the pile.

"Cities all over the world," Ben pointed out as he and Zack unfolded another map.

"Yeah, we've even been to some of these cities," Zack said.

Kevin fingered through the stack of unfolded maps, calling out the places their family had visited. "Colorado, San Francisco, New York, and Mom said we were going to London this summer."

"We've been to some of those places too," Ben said. "I wonder what it means."

"What about this place?" Zack held up one of the maps. "How do you even pronounce it?"

"Thessaloniki," Carly said. "It's in Greece."

"Well, I've never heard of it." Zack returned the map to the stack.

"Not surprising." Carly rolled her eyes as she picked up the journal and ran her hand across the embossed cover. She opened the book and leafed through the pages. "You guys, the handwriting changes in the middle of the journal. The last half looks like my dad's writing, but do any of you recognize the writing at the beginning?" Carly showed them the obvious difference between the handwriting in the book. "There's an odd slant to the lettering in the first pages of the journal," she pointed out. "The person who wrote this may be left-handed."

"It doesn't look familiar to me," Zack said.

Ben shook his head.

"I've never seen that writing before," Kevin said. "Do you really think this stuff has anything to do with their disappearance?"

"It must, we just have to figure out how to use it. All this stuff may tell us where they are," Ben replied.

They rifled through the rest of the maps, hoping to find something to guide them.

Zack took The Lincoln from his pocket and, gripping it in his hand, tried to will the blue light to return. *What were you trying to tell m*e? he kept repeating to himself.

"That thing shined pretty bright; does it give off any heat?" Kevin asked, interrupting Zack's concentration.

"No, it's not hot at all," Zack said, disappointed he wasn't able to get the penny to do what it had when they'd found it. "Actually, it feels kind of cold."

He passed The Lincoln to Kevin and watched him rub the coin between his fingers, then smell both the penny and his fingers.

Kevin shrugged and placed it on the table. "It smells normal."

"Does anyone have a penny?" Zack asked.

"I do." Carly dug into her pocket and pulled out a few coins. She selected a penny and put it down on the coffee table next to The Lincoln.

"The backs of these pennies are different," Ben said.

"This one has a picture of the Lincoln Memorial," Carly said. "And The Lincoln has the words 'one cent' with leafy things on the sides. Other than that, I don't see any difference between them."

Zack looked at the back of the coins. "How do you know that building is the Lincoln Memorial?"

"Because we went there when we visited Washington, DC," Carly told him.

Ben pushed the coins together. "Look at the color," he said. "Even though The Lincoln is older, it looks brand new compared to the other one."

"That's because my dad has had it in his watch where no one could touch it," Kevin said.

"Except me," Zack said. "At the party I touched it, and it gave me a shock so strong I thought my arm was going to fall off." He looked at the black dot that was still on his fingertip.

"It's not shocking any of us now," Carly pointed out.

"No, it's not," Zack acknowledged.

"Maybe it had something to do with the watch," Kevin said.

"Maybe." Zack put Carly's penny in one hand and The Lincoln in the other, comparing the weight of the coins. "They feel the same. What do you think?" he asked, passing both coins to Ben.

Ben held the coins in the same way. "I'm not sure," he replied.

"Kevin, go get Mom's kitchen scale," Zack instructed. "Maybe weighing them will tell us something."

Kevin left the guesthouse and returned, placing the scale on the table. Zack weighed each coin. Carly's penny weighed 2.5 grams. The Lincoln weighed 4.4 grams.

"Wow, the difference between this penny and The Lincoln is huge," Zack said, pointing at the penny on the table.

Ben looked at the scale with The Lincoln still on it. "That's a big difference all right, but what does that tell us?"

"Can't say that I know," Zack replied, turning his focus to the maps laid out on the table. "But what I do know is that all of these things are connected."

Carly picked up the journal again, and after an hour of making no headway in understanding what was written, she rubbed her eyes.

"I have to go to bed. My brain stopped working hours ago."

"It stopped working way before that," Zack mumbled.

"You're real funny," she said, making a face and heading for the door.

It was after midnight when the boys agreed that they would begin again in the morning. Zack suggested putting the maps and journal into the guesthouse safe.

"Your dad kept these things hidden, so I don't think we should just leave them lying around."

Ben agreed.

CHAPTER SEVEN

COMMAND CENTER

Carly

Carly opened her eyes and for one disorienting moment, wasn't sure where she was. It wasn't long before the memory of the previous day came flooding back, covering her with a familiar blanket of sadness. She couldn't help but quietly sob, thinking of similar mornings when she woke up and for a split-second, thought that her mom was still alive, only to soon realize that wasn't the case.

As she lay there, her mind cleared, and her helplessness turned to anger. *No!* She swung her legs over the side of the bed. *Dad is not dead.* With determination that she hadn't felt in a long time, she shook off the gloom and was ready to do whatever it took to find her dad. She quickly dressed, brushed her teeth, and threw her hair into a ponytail before heading to the guesthouse.

The smell of breakfast hit her at the top of the stairs. She tried to remember the last time she had eaten as she continued down the stairs, where in the dining room, Aunt Tina had laid out a huge breakfast spread.

"Good morning," Aunt Tina said with an exuberance Carly didn't expect. "We were just going to wake you."

On the table was a large stack of pancakes, a pile of bacon, a bowl of fruit, a pitcher of orange juice, and an egg dish Aunt Tina called a frittata, which she assured Carly contained no meat. A ravenous noise came from Carly's stomach.

"Come in and sit down," Aunt Tina told her. "Kevin went out to get the boys." The French doors opened and the boys stampeded toward the smell of food. "Here they are. Grab a seat now; go ahead and start without us," Aunt Tina said before joining Sharon in the other room.

"You guys look like you haven't slept," Carly whispered.

"We haven't," Ben said as they pushed past one another to pile their plates with food.

"Did you find anything?" she asked.

"Nothing yet. There's a lot of work to do. We need to hurry," he replied.

That was all that needed to be said. With their plates full, they began shoveling food into their mouths. It reminded Carly of a disgusting hot dog-eating contest she had seen on TV where contestants crammed hot dogs into their mouths as fast as they could. She thought it was repulsive at the time, and now here she was doing the same thing with her breakfast. *At least I'm not eating hot dogs!*

Sharon and Aunt Tina came into the dining room as the four of them were getting up from the table. Aunt Tina began to insist they sit back down and enjoy more breakfast, but saw all of the plates had been picked clean. Only one strawberry remained, and as her eyes fell upon it, Zack picked it up and popped it into his mouth.

"Would you like us to clear the table, Mom?" Zack asked after a loud belch.

Sharon looked at him unfazed. "No, honey, we'll do it."

Aunt Tina stared at the table and her jaw dropped. Carly heard her mumble something about vultures. "Sharon, let's go make you some toast."

++++++++++

"Welcome to the Command Center," Zack said, spreading his arms as they entered the guesthouse.

One wall was covered with a large corkboard, which already had one of the maps pinned to it. *How did they get that out of the house without waking everyone?* Carly wondered. The monitor from Kevin's room was sitting on the small desk against the wall, wired to a hard drive and ready to go. Pens, pencils, large and small notebooks, and paper for the printer replaced the DVDs on the bookcase in the corner.

"I can't believe you guys did all this!" Carly exclaimed, impressed at the accomplishments of their all-nighter.

"We couldn't sleep, so we thought we might as well be productive," Ben said. "We even fixed my tire."

"You must be wiped out," Carly said.

"For sure," Ben yawned. "We woke Kevin up, and he took care of the computer. Since then, we've mainly been concentrating on the maps. Some of these maps are so old they're completely outdated."

"Then why did they need to be kept hidden?" Carly asked.

"That's the question."

"Kevin," Zack interrupted. "We need you to start entering all of the map locations into the computer and see what you can come up with." Zack looked at Carly. "The journal is what we need you to work on." He pointed at the bookcase. "Use whatever you need."

"Where did you get all of this stuff?" Carly asked, examining the things on the shelves.

"I raided my mom's school supply cabinet. With only six weeks left of school, she won't even notice this stuff missing." Zack yawned.

Carly grabbed the journal, along with a spiral notebook, and sat down at the small kitchen table. Zack and Ben focused on the maps, while Kevin took a seat in front of the computer.

Carly opened the journal and copied "TRUST NO ONE," just as it was written, wondering what their dads had gotten themselves into that would call for such a warning. Hours passed as she stared at the pages of the journal, finding the rows of letters and numbers to be as baffling as they had been the night before. But when she came across a section at the top of one of the pages, something clicked.

I know what this is. It looked like the same code she and her friends had used in seventh grade to ensure that no one could read their texts to one another.

Underneath where she had written TRUST NO ONE, she wrote out the alphabet with the corresponding numbers beneath the letters.

Starting with the number one for the letter A, she assigned a consecutive number to every letter in the alphabet.

A B C D E F G H I J K L M N O P Q R S T U V W X Y Z
1 2 3 4 5 6 7 8 9 10 11 12 13 14 15 16 17 18 19 20 21 22 23 24 25 26

She then reversed the sequence.

Z Y X W V U T S R Q P O N M L K J I H G F E D C B A
1 2 3 4 5 6 7 8 9 10 11 12 13 14 15 16 17 18 19 20 21 22 23 24 25 26

It was a slow process, but using these letter and number combinations, she was able to decipher small sections throughout the journals.

"I think I've figured it out," she announced. "Well, part of it anyway."

Ben, Zack, and Kevin joined her around the kitchen table, where she laid out the journal and the notebook she used.

"What I was able to work out must not be very important, because the type of secret writing they used is pretty basic," Carly said.

"Then why use a code at all?" Kevin asked.

"I don't know. There were only small sections in the book that I could decipher," she told him. "I'm going to need a page from the journal scanned and emailed to me so that I can keep working on it, but for now here's what I found."

14 9 7 19 12 14 26 8 12 9 2 18 1 18 25 15 6 3 15 14 7 18 5 19 19 13 14 5

M R T H O M A S L I B R A R Y O F C O N G R E S S M A D E

1 16 16 15 9 14 20 13 5 14 20 1 9 12 9 14 3 15 12 14 14 26 9 24 19 Z Z R V U

A P P O I N T M E N T A S L I N C O L N M A R C H 1 1 9 5 6

Zack looked at what she had written. "What exactly have you figured out? This looks more confusing than before you started."

"Look closer," she told him as she transcribed her findings onto a separate piece of paper.

MR. THOMAS

LIBRARY OF CONGRESS

MADE APPOINTMENT AS LINCOLN

MARCH 1, 1956

"Everything I was able to decipher refers to dates at the Library of Congress and meetings with a Mr. Thomas. It looks like someone met with him at the library every single day, except Sundays, for over two months."

"Still not getting it," Zack said. "What do we care about meetings that took place in 1956?"

"I'm not sure that they did all take place in 1956," Carly replied.

"Now I'm confused," Kevin said.

"Look at this journal." Carly pointed to the first page. "The ink in the beginning is faded so much you can barely read it. Now compare it to the last entries, where the ink is fresh. These entries were definitely not all written within a few weeks of each other."

Ben looked closely at the journal. "I could swear that this is Dad's writing, but he was born in the 70s, so he couldn't have written this in 1956."

"Maybe he was researching some event that took place on that date at the Library of Congress," Kevin said.

"Then why all the secrecy?" Carly asked. "Does the name Mr. Thomas sound familiar to you guys?"

"No," Kevin replied.

"I can't say I recall Dad ever mentioning a Mr. Thomas," Ben said.

Carly looked at Zack, waiting for him to respond, and noticed a strange look on his face.

"I don't know anything about Mr. Thomas, but I'm starting to get a funny feeling," he said. He thought about it for a moment and pounded his fist on the table. "Actually, I think I've got it!"

WELCOME TO THE MACHINE

Zack

Zack jumped up and grabbed a pad of paper off the bookshelf. "I think I've got it!" he repeated. He began scribbling down the equations, struggling to keep up with the images streaming through his mind. Not understanding any of it.

"Got what?" Kevin asked, watching Zack write faster than he had ever seen.

Zack tore the page from the pad and reviewed what he had written. Satisfied, he handed the paper to Kevin. "I'm not exactly sure what this is, but it's something. See what you can find on these numbers."

Kevin sat in front of the computer. "Where are you getting this stuff from?" he asked Zack as he typed in the information. Zack didn't answer. "This is strange," Kevin said, his eyes on the monitor. "The first group of numbers is the speed of light and the second one . . ." He paused, waiting for the computer to give him the information. ". . . Has something to do with electromagnetic fields."

Zack hit himself on the head with the heel of his palm. "That's what it was trying to tell me!" he shouted. He jumped up, waving his hands in the air as he paced around the room. "Of course, the numbers that were between the math problems were years: 1954, 1960, 1962. I can't believe I didn't get it till now!"

"Get what?" Carly questioned.

"All of the information that the blue light gave me. It all makes sense," Zack said, his mind going a million miles a minute.

"What are you talking about?" Ben asked.

Zack forced himself to stop moving and answer the question. "When we found The Lincoln in the street, a blue light carried mathematical equations to me and showed me how easy it was to figure out the answers."

"Why didn't the rest of us see that?" Carly's tone was skeptical.

"Don't know," Zack replied.

"Wait, stop right there. Am I hearing you right? You… math… easy?"

"Yeah, exactly," Zack said, finding it hard to believe himself.

"Just when you think things couldn't get any weirder." Ben shook his head.

"Oh, it gets weirder," Zack assured him. "That math stuff wasn't the only thing the blue light showed me. There was something else that I couldn't understand, something about The Lincoln. The blue light gave me the answer. I just didn't know what the question was—until now."

"Will you please tell us what you're talking about?" Carly demanded.

"This coin contains energy, I mean crazy amounts of energy," Zack said, holding out The Lincoln in his hand. "The type of energy that will give us the power to time travel."

"What?" Kevin squinted and shook his head.

"Time travel! Have you completely lost it?" Carly questioned.

"Yeah man, you're crazy," Ben said, waving off what he was hearing.

"Just hear me out." Zack looked each of them in the eye. "You were in the street and you saw the bubble that formed around us. That was our protection. That was the electromagnetic field." He waited for a response, but there were just blank stares. "Ben, you said it felt like we were moving, didn't you? I think you were right. I think we took our first trip and didn't even know it."

"How do you figure that?" Ben asked.

"Because it told me," Zack said.

"Who told you?" Carly leaned forward.

"The blue light," Zack said, annoyed at the question. "Keep up! Aren't you paying attention?"

"I'm paying attention," Kevin said. "And I don't know what you're talking about either."

Zack held up The Lincoln. "This little penny is what I'm talking about. It's going to take us to find our dads. That has to be the reason they sent it to us!"

Ben, Carly, and Kevin glanced at each other, raising their eyebrows. Zack saw them looking at him like he was nuts, but it didn't deter his excitement.

"Kevin," Zack said, "we'll need something to tap into that energy. If I tell you what The Lincoln is capable of, can you build something that could handle that kind of power?"

"You're kidding, right?" Kevin replied. "If what you're saying is true, no one would be able to do what you're asking."

"You're wrong," Zack told him. "All you have to do is build something that can direct The Lincoln to certain places, dates, and times. That must be what Dad's watch could do and it wasn't some big high-tech piece of machinery."

Zack could see Kevin considering what he'd said.

"I've never done anything like that before, and I'm not sure it would work," Kevin replied.

"But you can put something together, right?" Zack asked, knowing that out of the four of them, Kevin was the only one with a remote chance of being able to do it. *Let's see what you're made of, Mr. Computer Science Contest Winner,* Zack thought. "If Dad's watch could do it, you've got to be able to come up with something."

Ben and Carly sat silent, watching Zack manipulate his little brother into doing what he wanted.

"You'll take a shot at it, won't you? I mean, you are willing do whatever it takes to find Dad, aren't you?" Zack added.

"Of course, but I can't promise it will work," Kevin replied. "I've never done anything like this."

"Yeah, yeah, you've said that already," Zack said as he began writing down more numbers.

"Let me get as much information as I can on what you've given me." Kevin turned to his computer and began surfing.

"Here." Zack handed him another piece of paper.

"This is not possible!" Carly said.

"Oh really?" Zack was so exhilarated he could barely contain himself. "Was it possible for The Lincoln to show up out of nowhere and put on a big laser show while holding us glued to the ground? Not to mention the whole math thing. You were there, you tell me."

"Okay, okay," she said, "I guess it's possible, but what do you expect us to do, build a time machine?"

Why, of all people, do I have to be stuck with HER during this freaking nightmare? Zack threw his hands up, not saying what he was really thinking. "Look, I don't expect *you* to do anything," he said. "If you don't want to take part in what we're about to do, get out of the way, 'cause I don't have time to listen to your usual negative crap. Our dads are missing and I'm sure these maps, the journal, and this coin are going to help us find them."

"Give me a break!" she defended. "I've had my head wrapped around these journals all day, and now out of the blue you're talking about time travel. You have to admit that it's pretty out there."

"Trust me, I'm not making this up," Zack assured her. "We need to find something we can turn into a time machine. It needs to be small enough to hide and programmable so that we can input dates and locations." He paced back and forth.

"Why don't you try a watch like your dad's?" Carly suggested.

"I don't think we're going to be able to find a pocket watch that can hold The Lincoln very easily, and we can't waste a bunch of time looking for one," Zack replied.

"Okay, what then?" Carly asked.

"How about our phone or a tablet or maybe a GPS?" Ben said.

"Yes!" Kevin exclaimed. "A GPS machine would be perfect. Tablets and phones have too much other stuff on them that could get in the way. Let me check something." He began a new search on his computer and took some time to review the information on the screen before turning to the others. "Let's go."

"Go where?" Carly asked.

"The Plug and Jalopy Joy," Kevin answered. He turned back to his computer and copied some numbers from the monitor onto his phone.

"His home away from home," Zack commented.

"We're going to build a time machine out of what we can get at Plug Electronics?" Carly asked sarcastically.

"We're only building a steering mechanism—The Lincoln will provide the power," Zack explained.

"What's at Jalopy Joy?" Ben asked.

Kevin pointed at the images on the monitor. "Those panels are used for firewalls in cars to reflect away heat. I'm not sure if we'll need it, but if we get a GPS to move at the speed of light I think we better have some kind of heat shield to protect the inside of it. Jalopy Joy may not even have those panels, but it's worth checking out."

Zack led the way up to the main house and opened the door. "Mom, we're going to the store. We'll be right back," he yelled.

"You're not going anywhere," she replied. "And lower your voice. I'm right here."

Zack ignored his mother's response.

"We're going to the Plug and we'll be right back," he said slowly, as if she hadn't understood him.

"Did you hear what I said? You guys are not leaving this house on your own. I'll drive you later, after Aunt Tina leaves."

"Okay, let me get this straight," Zack said. "You're not going to let us out of this house by ourselves?" He paused, folding his arms. "For how long? Are you going to let us go back to school next week?"

"I'm not sure," his mother answered.

"Really, Mom, there's four of us—nothing bad is going to happen. Besides, you can't protect us forever."

She stared at his face, contemplating what he'd said. "Zack, this is really not the time to challenge me." She rubbed her temples.

He took a deep breath and spoke calmly. "Kevin wants to go to the electronics store and we need to keep him occupied. We have the whole week off from school. We can't sit here and do nothing for the entire time."

She hesitated and took a deep breath. "All right, but afterwards I want you to come straight home. Don't stop anywhere else, you got it?"

"We'll be right back," he assured his mother as they moved toward the door.

"Do you have your debit card?"

"Kevin has his," Zack answered.

"Do you have your phone?" she asked.

"Yes, Mother."

"Is it charged?"

"Yes, Mother," Zack said in a mocking tone, rolling his eyes.

"I mean it, don't be gone long," she told him.

+++++++++++

Carly

Carly jumped off of Ben's bike when they turned into their driveway, and after getting her bike from the garage, they hurried to the strip mall where Plug Electronics and Jalopy Joy were two of the many stores sandwiched between the grocery store and the bank. They parked their bikes and walked into the Plug. Zack and Ben lingered at the cell phone display, while Carly followed Kevin to the area reserved for computer accessories.

"Hey, Kevin, congratulations!" the clerk said, referring to the computer science contest. "I believe that makes you the youngest winner."

"Yeah, thanks," Kevin replied as he and Carly approached the counter. "I need something for a new project I'm working on." He looked at the numbers he had put in his phone. "Do you have the PE 6000 GPS/Sonar Combo in stock?"

"That's last year's model. I might have one in the back," the clerk said, moving toward the stockroom. "That sonar detects objects underwater. Are you going fishing or hunting for treasure?"

Kevin glanced over at Carly. "I guess you could say we'll be doing both."

The clerk returned with two of the devices Kevin requested and placed them on the counter. Kevin opened one of the boxes and pulled out the GPS device. To the right of the five-inch screen was a toggle knob with four buttons. Attached to the GPS was a mount that served as a stand, allowing it to sit upright on its own. Kevin nodded his head in approval.

"I'll take them both," he said.

Zack and Ben joined them at the counter to inspect the GPS Kevin chose.

"Why this one?" Ben asked.

"I'll show you later," Kevin told him, handing the clerk his debit card.

How's he going to transform that into a time machine? Carly thought as she watched the GPS machines being put into a bag.

They walked down a few doors to the auto parts store, where Kevin described what they needed.

"I have just the thing," the salesperson told them. They followed the man down a few aisles, where he pointed out a heavy-duty, stainless-steel mesh with a ceramic inner pad designed to protect car engines from extreme heat conditions that occur during racing. "It can be customized to any size or shape," he told them.

"That's perfect," Kevin beamed.

++++++++++

Zack

The pizza delivery guy was walking back to his car as they rode up the driveway of the Marshall home. They leaned their bikes against the side of the house, and Zack opened the gate. He looked around to make sure the coast was clear for them to drop off their sizable bags before going up to the main house.

"Oh, good, you're home," Sharon said, as they entered through the French doors. "Did you have any problems?"

"No, I told you we'd be all right," Zack replied.

"You kids wash your hands and pull down some plates, please," Sharon said as she opened one of the pizza boxes.

"Can we take ours out to the guesthouse?" Zack asked.

"No, I want us to have dinner together tonight," Sharon replied.

There was a collective sigh of disappointment. They were all anxious for Kevin to get started.

"Where's Aunt Tina?" Kevin asked, getting glasses out of the cabinet.

"She had to go home, but she'll be back in a couple of days." Sharon doled out salad from the plastic container.

The occasional fork colliding with a plate was the only sound heard during dinner. When the pizza boxes were empty, Zack noticed the drained glass of wine next to his mother's untouched plate of food.

Sharon spoke in a somber voice. "I want you kids to know that wherever your fathers are right now, I'm sure they're trying to get home. I want us all to have faith that they'll return soon."

Feeling the weight of her words, they all nodded. Her statement only added to their sense of urgency. Zack saw the worry on his mom's face. *I wish Aunt Tina had stayed. We don't have time to babysit her tonight.*

++++++++++

After helping to clear the table, they returned to the guesthouse, where Kevin immediately got to work collecting the tools and supplies he needed from the garage. He covered the kitchen table with white paper to set up his workstation in the same way he began all his projects. Zack knew there was nothing Kevin enjoyed more than taking apart some electronic gizmo and making it perform in ways it was never intended. He saw Kevin's eyes light up when he disassembled one of the GPS devices and began examining its interior.

Using the information Zack provided, Kevin worked well into the night. Zack watched Kevin's brain working at full power, which only drove home how badly he himself had been betrayed by their family genetics. *How does he know this stuff? He's just a kid.* Zack was amazed at Kevin's determination, focus, and precision as he watched from the side, wishing he could help.

CHAPTER NINE

YOU CAN'T MAKE ME

Carly

THUD! Carly bolted upright only to realize she must have fallen asleep on the guesthouse couch. In the darkness, she could barely make out Kevin lying on the floor, grabbing his head as he winced in pain. "Are you all right?" she whispered.

"Yes," he replied, half-asleep. "I banged my head on the table."

Carly reached for her phone, then remembered it was still at the gymnastics studio.

"What time is it?" she asked.

"Three thirty in the morning," he replied quietly.

She knew Kevin hadn't been asleep for very long, because he was still working on the GPS when she had dozed off around one o'clock.

"Do you want to trade places? I'll take the floor," she offered, noticing that Ben and Zack were gone, probably asleep in their rooms.

"Thanks, but I need to get back to work," he replied.

"It's too early." She yawned, resting her head back on the couch.

Kevin got up and made his way to the chair next to her. "Carly," he whispered. "I'm scared."

She sat up and turned to him. "Of what?"

"This time machine I'm building; it just might work."

She laughed, then covered her mouth, not wanting to wake Ben and Zack. "Isn't that the point?"

"Yes, but I think we're opening the door to something very dangerous. Time is not supposed to move backward. Transporting a human body back in time defies nature," he said with his head down, wringing his hands. "What if something goes wrong?"

"You're going to have to trust that your brother is not leading us toward disaster." She paused and shook her head. "I can't believe I just told you to trust Zack."

"I can't believe it either, and I'm not so sure that I can," he said, sounding panicky. "I think the best thing that can happen is that when I'm finished, the GPS doesn't work. Then I'll be off the hook."

Carly could hear how distressed he was. "Oh yeah, like you should hope for failure," she said, rejecting the notion. "You're not on any hook. It's not like we're doing this for fun. We're all willing to face whatever danger comes up in order to help our dads, right? Getting the GPS to work is only the first step. We'll have to deal with what that brings when we get that far."

"Easy for you to say," he said, sounding a little better.

"I'm serious."

"I know you are. Thanks." He stood and headed toward the kitchen.

Carly's head sank back into the pillow on the couch, and she was asleep within seconds.

++++++++++

The sound of Zack's obnoxious voice was the next thing she heard. "There's nothing that connects these things," he said, sounding frustrated.

Carly opened her eyes, squinting from the bright sunlight that filled the room. She could see Zack and Ben at each end of the coffee table examining a map, and she rolled over.

"About time," she heard Zack say.

"What time is it?" she asked, her face buried in the pillow.

"Eleven," Ben answered.

She lifted her head. "Eleven?" She slowly sat up and looked toward the kitchen. "Hey Kevin, you okay?"

"Mm-hmm," he replied, not taking his eyes off of his work.

"I'll be back." Carly slowly got to her feet and headed to the main house.

She returned within a half hour to find the others in the same position. She sat down on the couch and slid the journal near her, where she sat analyzing page after page.

Hours passed, and the room was completely silent when Kevin replaced the last screw. "That should do it."

With a rush of excitement, Carly quickly went to the kitchen with Ben and Zack on her heels. She was surprised to see that the outside of the navigation device looked the same as it had before he'd started. Kevin had installed a hinge on the GPS/Sonar Combo to allow it to open like a clam. Inside, a makeshift heat shield covered the interior, with a small chamber reserved for The Lincoln.

"Are we going to have to subscribe to a navigational service for the GPS?" Ben asked.

"No. Depending on how far in the past we go, I couldn't be sure that a service would be available. That's why I chose this model. I've rigged it so that the GPS draws enough power from a small battery to allow me to program the time, date, and location by turning the toggle knob."

"When I press this," he pointed to the button beneath the toggle knob, "it should engage The Lincoln and then we'll see. I haven't tried it yet, but if this coin really does have the power that Zack says it does, the GPS machine will be able to harness that energy to get us to any time and place that we program into it."

"Oh, don't worry, The Lincoln has the power all right," Zack said as he examined the GPS, nodding with approval.

"I think our first trip should be to see Mr. Thomas the day after the last entry in the journal," Carly said.

"What do you mean *our* first trip?" Zack questioned. "You and Kevin are staying here, just in case something bad happens."

"What?" Carly narrowed her eyes. She got up and stomped over to Zack. "Oh no! That's not how it's going to be." She waved her finger in Zack's face. "I'm not just going to sit here while you're gone, wondering if you guys are ever coming back. No way!"

"Dad would kill me if I let you risk your life," Ben told her.

"I'm going with you, end of story," she stated and turned her back to them, not willing to hear any more about it.

"I built it and you can't stop me from going," Kevin cried. "You'd better let me come with you, or I'm telling Mom exactly what you're doing."

Ben looked at Zack. "I told you they wouldn't take no for an answer."

Zack shook his head. "Okay, I guess we don't have a choice."

"All right then," Carly said with satisfaction. "We should try getting to 1956. That's the year that keeps coming up in the journal. Then we can focus on trying to reach this Mr. Thomas person."

They all nodded in agreement.

"At no time can my mom find out about what we're doing, or we can kiss finding our dads goodbye," Zack said. "She doesn't usually come back here after dinner, so I think that's the best time to go."

"Why can't we just set the time of our return for the same time we left? That way no one would know we were ever gone," Carly asked.

"Good question," Kevin said.

"Because time keeps moving forward, and if we returned at the same time we left, it may only be a few hours, but it would still be in the past," Zack explained, then stopped. His eyebrows pulled together and he cocked his head.

"What's the matter?" Ben asked.

"I'm not sure how I knew that. I mean, the words just came out of my mouth."

"I don't like this," Ben said with his eyes fixed on Zack.

"I do," Carly said. "He finally sounds like he knows something."

Kevin snorted back a laugh and sat down in front of the computer. Zack didn't say a word. He was still looking confused when he and Ben returned their attention to the maps.

They sat in silence for half an hour, which seemed like an eternity.

"Wow," Carly said, drawing everyone's attention. "Tonight, we're going to do something that a few days ago we would've thought to be impossible."

"We'll see," Ben said under his breath.

"What time is it?" Carly asked.

"Wear a watch already!" Zack yelled. "It's ten minutes since the last time you asked."

"This is the longest day ever," Kevin said. "Let's go get my mom moving on dinner," he told Carly.

++++++++++

Zack

"Mom knows something's up," Kevin said as the four of them returned to the guesthouse, having had dinner.

"She does not! You're paranoid," Zack told him. "Why would she be suspicious, because we were hungry? I don't think so."

Kevin raised his eyebrows. "If you say so," he conceded as he took the chair in front of his computer and Carly sat down on the couch. Ben flopped down in one of the leather chairs.

Zack picked up the GPS and slowly paced back and forth. "If I'm correct, this machine will be able to transport us all safely, as long as we're holding on to this handle." He pointed at the bracket on the navigational device that would normally be used to mount it in a vehicle. He glanced over and saw Ben with his lips pressed together.

"What?" Zack asked.

"I've gone along with this ridiculous idea to build a time machine without saying anything, but now you're scaring me. I can see you really think this will work and I want to believe you, but the thing is, the Zack I've known my entire life—no offense—would never be able to pull this off. Either this is something that's never going to work or you're not who we think you are. Maybe something happened to the real Zack when we found the coin and were blinded by the light."

"Are you kidding?" Zack asked. "You want me to prove that I'm myself?"

"Just answer one question," Ben said. "What did my dad give your dad for his birthday?"

Zack wasted no time answering Ben's question. "A steel penny. Did I pass the test?"

"Yeah man, but you can't blame me—you haven't been yourself."

"I am myself!" Zack insisted. "I told you I got all this from the blue light. Do you think I could have come up with this on my own?"

"That's my point," Ben stressed. "Either way, it's hard to believe."

Zack's voice rose in frustration. "Look, I don't know why all of this was dumped on me. I never asked for it, that's for sure! Ever since we found The Lincoln, my head has been filled with numbers and all kinds of weird stuff." His voice broke and his shoulders slumped forward. "This thing is going to work. It just has to."

"Well, we're about to find out, aren't we?" Ben said.

Zack nodded. "That's right. If everything goes as planned, the GPS will be powered by The Lincoln. That bubble that formed around us in the street is the electromagnetic force field that will protect us from whatever's out there that could hurt us."

"Like particles in the atmosphere, heat, and radiation?" Kevin asked.

"Yeah, stuff like that," Zack replied. "The force of energy and the speed that we'll be traveling should stop us from letting go, but to make sure that we don't become separated from the GPS, I want each of you to tie this around your wrist." He handed out six-inch strips of copper wire enclosed in clear pliable plastic. "The Lincoln should recognize the copper going though these as a sort of lightning rod and direct energy through it."

"We've got to wear these things?" Carly asked as they all tied the cable around their wrists. "We look like we just escaped from being held hostage in a stereo store."

"It's not a fashion statement. If you don't like it, come up with something better," Zack told her. "Kevin, what did you program into the GPS?"

"May 12, 1956, 2:00 p.m., and 101 Independence Avenue, SE, Washington, DC."

"Good," Zack said. "When we get there, we'll need to hide the GPS right away. If I can't do it, you need to take the coin out and put the time machine in my backpack," he told Kevin. "Let's try not to draw attention to ourselves."

Kevin and Carly nodded.

"This is your last chance to back out," he continued. "I'm not really sure what's going to happen. So, if you're having second thoughts, you can just wait here for me."

"No way. I'm not waiting. I'm in," Carly said.

"Me too," Ben added.

"Let's go," Kevin said.

They stood in the living room of the guesthouse. Ben, Kevin, and Carly each put one hand on the mount of the GPS that now served as a handle. Zack placed The Lincoln in the device and closed it. He positioned himself next to the others and took hold of the mount. Butterflies filled his stomach, and his heart raced as he pressed the button.

The GPS began to vibrate, and a painful ringing sound caused them to tighten their grip. Zack was the first to notice the iridescent purple line. Like a churning liquid, it poured around them. A film sprung from it and enclosed around them. Beams of light shot out from the GPS in every direction, followed by a bright light. They buried their faces in their free arms before they began to spin. Held together by centrifugal force, the ground dropped away from their feet.

They were gone.

CHAPTER TEN

THE FIRST TIME

Carly

Carly, Ben, Zack, and Kevin held on to the GPS for dear life, screaming as they plummeted to the earth. The bubble that protected them disappeared, and they were thrown onto grass surrounded by three large pine trees that concealed their arrival. Disoriented and a bit queasy, it took a few seconds for them to get their bearings.

"You have reached your destination," proclaimed the voice from the GPS.

"Hey nimrod, you didn't deactivate the lady's voice. We can't have her going off every time we land someplace," Zack told Kevin as he looked around, making sure he hadn't lost the others. "I thought you put in the address of the Library of Congress."

"Where are we?" Ben asked.

Kevin didn't reply. He was busy vomiting between two of the trees. "Make a note, never eat before you time travel," he choked, with his head between his knees.

Carly breathed in the smell of pine and freshly cut grass before moving toward Kevin who was white as a ghost.

"Kevin looks bad. We need to get him some water or something. Maybe we can find a store," she told the others, patting Kevin's shoulder. "You'll be all right."

"I was wrong," Ben announced, holding his arm out. "Zack, you did it. I have to hand it to you, man, that was amazing!"

Zack smacked Ben's hand and pointed at him. "I told you it would work, but I have to say, that was way cooler than I thought it would be." He grabbed the GPS and removed The Lincoln before putting it into his backpack. "We should be able to find our dads in no time with this thing."

Carly peered through the opening between the trees and saw a large building that looked like a Greek temple. "We're definitely not at the Library of Congress," she announced.

"Kevin, are you good to go?" Zack asked.

"Yeah," he croaked, wiping his mouth on his shirt.

"You built a time machine." Ben slapped Kevin on the back. "Man, that's impressive!"

Kevin winced, trying to keep the rest of his dinner from leaving his stomach.

Cautiously surveying their surroundings, they discretely left the seclusion of the pine trees, and walked around to the front of the building, craning their necks as their eyes followed the stairs leading to enormous white columns.

"What is this place?" Zack asked.

"The Lincoln Memorial," Carly replied. "The same building that's on the back of a penny."

She and Ben caught each other's eye, and Carly knew that they were both thinking the same thing. They had stood in practically the exact spot on their family visit to DC. Carly closed her eyes and could feel her mom's long, soft fingers still wrapped around her hand just as they had been on that day. Her head dropped forward, and it took all she had to push the memory aside. She knew not to let herself go to that familiar place of overwhelming sadness. *Not now.*

"Should we go up?" Kevin asked.

"I think so," Ben said. "There may be a reason we landed here." Zack nodded in agreement.

"Meet you up there," Ben said to Carly as he and Zack raced up the stairs, passing several groups of people on the immense staircase.

Kevin was a bit woozy and climbed the stairs slowly next to Carly.

"Kevin, this is crazy," she told him as she looked around at the men and women on the staircase at different stages of their visit to the memorial. "We're in Washington, DC," she said, still registering that only moments before, they'd been in California.

"I know," he replied. "We're actually walking around in 1956."

"See, you were worried for nothing," she assured him. "I knew you could do it."

"We still have to get home," he said with concern as they continued climbing.

When they finally reached Zack and Ben, they were drawn to the statue of Abraham Lincoln, amazed at the sculpture's massive size and the feeling of reverence that surrounded it. They made their way through the crowd to get a closer look at the enormous seated figure. Tourists parted as they passed, staring at their unusual appearance. Someone pointed to Zack's T-shirt.

"What kind of joke is that?" the man barked.

Zack looked down to see what he was talking about.

"Los Angeles Dodgers, like that would ever happen," the man said, with a huff. He pulled his daughter closer to him, as if Zack were dangerous, before walking away.

"The Dodgers must not have moved to LA yet," Ben whispered.

"They didn't leave Brooklyn till 1958," Zack replied.

"Sounds like that guy is in for a big surprise," Ben said.

"Him and a lot of other people," Zack agreed. They continued getting stares from the people keeping their distance. "It's not just this T-shirt; look at the way everyone is dressed. We definitely don't fit in," he whispered.

"If we're trying to go unnoticed, we're doing a poor job," Carly agreed, observing that Kevin was still white as a ghost. "Let's find a place to get Kevin some water."

"Yeah, let's get out of here," Ben said.

"Hang on," Zack replied, moving behind Ben and slipping his shirt over his head, he quickly put it back on inside out.

++++++++++

They descended the stairs, and as they walked, they took in their surroundings, noticing how different things were from what they were used to seeing. The cars were big and shiny with white wall tires. Some of them had curved roofs with rounded fenders. Others had flattened roofs with huge fins on the sides of the trunks. They were unsure if the bus line looked old-fashioned or futuristic.

A drinking fountain caught Carly's eye. "There." She pointed, and then wished she hadn't. *That thing looks disgusting.*

Kevin positioned himself over the fountain and pushed the button, desperately waiting for the arc of water to hit his mouth, but only a few dribbles seeped out of the hole. "Nothing," he said.

"You're probably better off," Carly commented.

There was a cool breeze, and the sun went behind a cloud. Carly looked up and noticed a line of dark gray clouds approaching.

"That looks pretty serious," Ben said, as his eyes followed hers.

"Sure does," Zack agreed.

They walked several blocks before seeing a sign on a building across the street.

"Look." Carly pointed at a storefront with the words "Soda and Candy" painted above the small awning. "Let's cross here."

The door to the store was propped open.

"I'll get you a water," Carly told Kevin, leaving the others to wait outside.

She entered the store, and looking around the compact surroundings, she saw that it was filled with everything from baby food to motor oil. Her stomach lurched when her eyes fell on the jars next to the old man behind the register. Whatever was in them took her mind back to dissecting a frog in biology class. Lined up on the counter were several creepy-looking dolls dressed in lace. Apparently, May is the time of year for kites, because there were quite a few on display. Carly's eyes went to the back of the room, where she expected to see a wall of refrigerators with glass doors, but instead found a red cooler. Inside the cooler was an assortment of small soda bottles.

"Excuse me," she said to the clerk. "Where do you keep the water?"

He looked at her, dumbfounded. "In the pipes."

She returned the same confused expression. "Where's that?"

"In the pipes, kid. Are you putting me on?" the man said angrily.

"My friend has an upset stomach, and I need to buy a bottle of water," she told him, assuming he didn't understand what she was asking.

"I do not sell water in a bottle, but if your friend is sick, you might do better with ginger ale." The man came from behind the counter. He selected a soda and opened it using the bottle opener attached to the side of the cooler, letting the cap fall to the floor.

"Ten cents," the clerk stated.

Carly dug into her pocket and pulled out a five-dollar bill. "This is the smallest I have," she said, putting the money on the counter. His eyes went straight to the speaker wire tied to her wrist, and she saw his demeanor change. He had a strange look on his face as he examined the five-dollar bill without touching it.

"I do not accept play money," he grumbled, pushing her money back toward her. "You should have told me you were a charity case from the start. Take the soda and be gone with you."

"Thank you," she said, realizing the five-dollar bill she'd handed him must have looked different than one from the '50s. She grabbed the ginger ale and practically ran outside.

"What took so long?" Ben asked. "I was just about to go in after you."

"I'm sure that guy thinks I'm crazy," she said.

"He's not the only one," Zack mumbled.

Carly forced her lips into a tight smile and gave Zack the evil eye as she handed the soda to Kevin, who guzzled down half of the bottle and belched.

"Let's go home. We aren't prepared enough to be here," Carly said. "We have no useable money, and our clothes are attracting way too much attention."

"Go home? We just got here," Zack protested. "There are a lot of things we need to check out."

He barely finished making his point when there was a loud crack. Startled by the noise, they looked up to see that the approaching clouds were now overhead. The rumbling sound of rolling thunder was deafening. It began to rain, and glimpses of lightning appeared in the dark sky. People were running for cover, while those with umbrellas struggled to keep them from being blown inside out. The four of them huddled underneath the awning of the store, trying to stay dry. They watched water inch its way up the curb, flooding the street. The store owner came out and glanced over at them as he removed the doorstop and disappeared back inside, leaving the door to slam shut.

"I guess you're right," Zack yelled to be heard over the rain. "We should go home. We're not going to get anything done in this mess."

"We have to get out of sight," Carly shouted. "The store owner was nice enough to give us a drink. I don't want to give him a heart attack from seeing us disappear into thin air."

"Let's go around the side of the building. We're going to get soaked, but we don't have a choice," Zack said.

Kevin programmed the device with the correct time of day and their address. After placing The Lincoln inside the GPS, they braced themselves for the deluge and took off running, gathering next to the side of the building. Zack turned his back to the wind, pulling the neck of his T-shirt up near his ears and bent over the device in an attempt to keep it dry. They each placed one hand on the handle and Kevin pushed the button.

Their eyes squinted as the painful ringing sound pierced their eardrums. The iridescent purple line and the film forming their protection took shape on top of the deepening puddle where they stood. Suddenly they began to spin, and the ground fell away from their feet; within seconds they fell to the ground.

++++++++++

"You have reached your destination," the voice announced.

Unsure of where they were, they slowly got up, inspecting themselves for injuries. In the darkness, it was hard to see through the trees and shrubs surrounding them.

"Everyone all right?" Zack called out.

Like roll call, Ben, Kevin, and Carly each answered back.

Carly realized she was no longer dripping wet. "Traveling at the speed of light is one way to dry your clothes," she commented.

Zack removed the coin from the device and looked around for something he recognized. "Kevin, what address did you put in this thing?"

"Ours," Kevin replied.

They heard the sound of nearby passing cars and froze.

"Follow that sound," Zack yelled.

After taking a few steps through the trees, they reached an opening.

"Where are we?" Carly asked before noticing a large wood sign that read, "Topanga Canyon."

"Look." Ben ran over to the remnants of caution tape tied to a tree and blowing in the wind.

"This is it!" Carly yelled as it dawned on her exactly where they were. "This is the lookout where I saw Dad and Bill."

"Where's Dad's car?" Ben asked, turning on the spot.

"The police must have had it taken away," Zack said.

"Why did we end up here?" Kevin questioned.

They wandered around, looking for something—anything—that might give them a clue about the men in the white van, but there was nothing to be found. Carly stood at the edge of the lookout and gazed out at the carpet of city lights spanning the valley floor.

"They're out there somewhere," she said quietly. The scene of their dads being held at gunpoint began playing over and over in her mind. She tried to be strong, but in the darkness, no one saw the tears streaming from her eyes.

"We'd better get home," Zack said. "It's getting late." They stood on the side of the road waiting for a break between cars. Finally, they were able to reach the clearing on the other side.

Carly looked at the path leading down the hill. "This is right where I was, and I couldn't get to them," she said. Her voice broke as she looked back across the street.

"Thank God!" Ben told her. "Or they would've taken you too."

"I should have done something," she replied, shaking her head.

"What could you have done? They had a gun," Kevin said.

Even Zack nodded in agreement. "Let's go," he said, and led the way down the path.

CHAPTER ELEVEN

GET IT TOGETHER

Zack

Zack turned the doorknob of the guesthouse, but the door wouldn't open. He leaned his shoulder in and gave it a shove. Nothing happened.

"Help me push," he mouthed to Kevin.

Kevin stood next to him and pushed as hard as he could. It still didn't budge. Even with the addition of Ben's weight, they only managed to get the door to open a few inches. They each squeezed through the small opening and took a few steps inside, walking on the debris scattered around the floor. Ben searched for the light switch and found it dangling from the wall.

"What happened in here?" Zack asked. In the darkness, he was barely able to make out the bookshelves that were now empty. The computer, television, and school supplies had all been dumped onto the floor.

Snap! Everyone stood still.

"Sorry." Carly lifted her foot off the broken pencil.

"There must have been an earthquake while we were gone," Ben surmised from the condition of the room.

"Earthquake?" Kevin yelled. "We've got to see if Mom is okay!" They all hurried out of the narrow opening and ran up to the main house. Zack opened the door and they rushed in.

"Mom!" he screamed. They stopped in their tracks when they saw everything in its place, and lights flickering from the far end of the house. *There definitely was not an earthquake*, Zack thought.

His mother came rushing into the room. "What's wrong? What happened?"

They just stood there with their eyes shifting from one to another, each waiting for the other to say something.

After a few seconds, Zack finally spoke up. "Umm, is there anything to eat?"

"Zack Marshall, you scared me half to death. What were you thinking?"

"I guess I'm just hungry," he replied.

"Well, that's no excuse. There's leftovers in the refrigerator," she told him. "And don't ever do that again." She left the room with her hand on her chest, shaking her head.

Zack nodded toward the kitchen, and Kevin went to the refrigerator, grabbing a plate covered with foil. Zack got a flashlight from the drawer, and they quickly went back to the guesthouse to assess the damage.

"I can't believe a coin could do all of this," Ben said as Zack shined the light across the littered floor.

The bedrooms were not disturbed, and nothing much had moved in the kitchen. Yet the living room from where they had departed was trashed. Everything in the room was on the floor and all the electrical sockets were pulled away from the wall. Zack turned off the electricity to the guesthouse so that he could put them back in place.

"Hold this for me," Zack said, handing Ben the flashlight. "These wires are copper. They were drawn to The Lincoln," Zack told them.

Carly's eyebrows pulled together. "How do you know that?"

Zack shrugged his shoulders as he screwed the last outlet cover back onto the wall before restoring the power.

Kevin's focus was the electronics. He picked up the hard drive and monitor and put them back on the desk. When his computer booted up, he sighed with relief. Ben and Zack returned the television to its upright position only to find it had not fared as well. It was dead.

"How are we going to explain that?" Kevin asked, pointing at the television.

"I don't know, but the next time we take off we'd better do it from outside," Zack advised.

Carly collected the school supplies littering the floor and returned them to the bookshelf. She surveyed the room to find only one thing still out of place. A baseball trophy of Zack's was wedged between the cushions of the couch.

"I can't believe that we could be that stupid," she said, as she began walking circles in the room.

"Yeah, but at least we didn't leave from the kitchen or we would have pulled out all the copper plumbing," Zack replied, returning the trophy to the shelf.

"I'm not talking about that," Carly practically yelled. "We need to be much better prepared if we are going to travel to the past. We need clothes, money, and maps. There's absolutely no technology in 1956 that we can count on. This is going to be way harder than we thought."

"You need to calm down, Sis," Ben responded, throwing himself into the chair.

"Yeah," Zack said, "It could've been worse."

"How?" Carly asked, putting her hand on her hip.

"One of us could have lost consciousness, or we could have arrived home without all of our body parts."

"Gross," she said. "That's disgusting."

"Don't kid yourself," Zack said. "It could've happened, or the whole thing might not have worked at all. So, I would say our first trip was a huge success."

"I never want to be in that position again." Carly picked up a notebook and made a list of everything they would require for their next expedition.

"I'll need to go by the house to get some supplies," she told Ben, "and I'll have to go to a couple of stores. Zack and Kevin, you guys bring any clothes you have that could have been worn in the 1950s and put them in the closet so I can sort them out."

"It's not like we have that many," Zack remarked.

"I'll deal with that after I see what you've got. Kevin, I'm going to need some copper wire," Carly said.

"How much?"

"It doesn't matter, whatever you have will do. I am going to bed now. There's a lot of work to do tomorrow," she said.

As the door shut behind her, Zack laughed. "I guess the old bossy Carly is back."

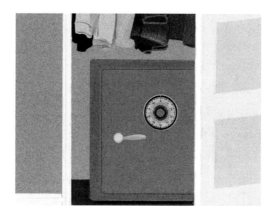

CHAPTER TWELVE

MONEY

Carly

T he morning sun poured into the room, spotlighting the notes Carly was reviewing as she lay on the bed. She was ready to take control. The thought of Bill Marshall having sent them The Lincoln to use for time travel was thrilling. No longer did she have to be a victim of things happening around her.

First, they would need replacements for the hideous speaker wire that they wore on their wrists. They also needed clothes. Her mind wandered for a moment. *Money.* Money was a big issue. They needed bills printed prior to the year in which they would be traveling. She remembered going with her dad to his favorite store, where he would buy collectable coins and small denominations of old bills. She dressed quickly and ran out to the guesthouse.

Ben was sitting on the chair with his leg dangling over the side and a glass of orange juice in his hand. Zack was lying on the couch with an opened soda on the coffee table next to him when Carly barged in and began asking questions.

"Ben, after the police went through the house, did you open the safe?"

"No," he said. "You were there when I checked to see if someone tried to force it open. Why?"

"Do you know what's in there?" she asked.

"Yeah, Dad's coin collection. Why?"

"We need money printed in the '40s or '50s. I've seen Dad buy bills like that. Do you think they're in the safe?"

"I don't know," Ben said. "Give me a chance to wake up and we'll go take a look."

Carly went for the yogurt and blueberries in the refrigerator and sat down at the table, allowing Ben fifteen minutes, which she felt was ample time. Although he didn't agree, he got dressed and followed her out the door.

+++++++++++

Ben and Carly reached their house and went straight to the office. The safe was substantial in size, taking up most of the closet where it was stored. Their dad had entrusted Ben with the combination, and after a few attempts, he questioned whether the series of numbers he was using were correct, but with one more try the door finally popped open.

Their eyes immediately fell on the small glass box big enough to hold only its contents, their mother's wedding rings. They stood there speechless, staring at the box. Carly remembered the day their mother talked to them about her rings. She was ill and had become so thin that she could no longer wear them on her finger. They dangled from a chain around her neck. She lifted the chain and separated the rings, telling Carly she hoped that the ring with the square diamond would someday be her wedding ring, and that Ben would have the platinum band enlarged to use as his. That way they would always have a part of her with them. The memory was so vivid it was as if it had happened yesterday. Carly watched through glassy eyes as Ben pushed the box out of view.

He reached his hand into the safe and removed a stack of wooden disks with a metal rod running through the middle, holding them all together.

"I thought this was a roll of coins," he said, smiling as he showed it to Carly. He was obviously trying to make light of the moment, and Carly went along.

"If it was, it would be the largest coins ever made." She laughed and sniffled at the same time, wiping the corners of her eyes.

Ben examined the disks. "These things turn," he said, spinning the wooden disks that moved independently of one another.

"What's that along the edges?" she asked.

"I don't know." He examined the random sequence of the letters and numbers that were stamped around the outermost parts of the disks.

Ben handed it to Carly, and she inspected the wooden balls on each end securing the metal rod in place, then spun the disks around, letting them stop on their own. "Maybe it's a game," she said as she handed it back to Ben. He returned it to the safe.

Ben shrugged his shoulders and focused his attention to what was on the shelves. Several small rectangular-shaped boxes could be seen, along with other boxes that were slightly bigger. He began taking them out and stacking them on the floor next to Carly.

"There's more in here," Ben said, looking deeper into the safe, "but let's check these out before we empty the whole thing."

Carly opened each box carefully so as not to disturb its contents. Half of the boxes contained coins, and the other half contained small denominations of bills dated from 1940 to 2000.

"There's thousands of dollars in here," Ben said.

"This is exactly what we need." Carly grinned. This was more than she had hoped for. "Do you think these have any value from a collector's standpoint?"

"Not the bills, they're not in very good condition." Ben fanned out a stack of five-dollar bills. "Wow, look how different these bills are from the ones we use now. The picture of Abraham Lincoln is so small."

Carly examined them closely. "They look weird. Do you think Dad will be angry if we use this money?"

"If he and Bill sent us The Lincoln, I think we can use whatever we need to try to find them."

"I'm going to take a good amount of this back to the Marshalls'. I don't want to keep coming back here every time we need money," she said.

Ben helped her select the denominations according to the series dates on the bills, and pulled some rolls of coins from a box that was dated 1950.

Carly went to her room to get clothes that would be appropriate for the '50s and instructed Ben to do the same. She looked around her room and realized how badly she wanted to come home. She wanted to snuggle under her blankets, sleep in her own bed, and use her own shower. But the one thing she wanted most of all was to see her dad when she went downstairs for breakfast. She grabbed the long-eared bunny from the stuffed animals on her bed and held it tightly in her arms. *Focus,* she told herself.

A cardigan sweater and capri pants were the only clothes she had that could be worn in the '50s. She put her laptop in its case and got down on the floor, pulling a toolbox from under the bed. She ran her hand over the top, wiping off the dust, as tears welled up in her eyes. Her mother was bedridden during the last few months of her life, and making jewelry was one of the few things they could still do together. Carly knew she had to be strong. If it weren't for their current situation, she would never be doing this. She opened the box, finding most of the supplies she would need to make the wristbands. She closed the lid and grabbed her things, carrying them downstairs with her bunny still tucked under her arm. Ben was waiting for her by the door.

+++++++++++

They raced through the street to the Marshalls' driveway and dropped their bikes on the side of the house.

"Here," Ben said, handing Carly her sweater that had fallen out of her bag.

They carried their stuff into the guesthouse, where they hung their '50s clothes in the closet alongside Kevin and Zack's. Carly wasted no time taking her jewelry-making supplies up to the room she was using, where she found the bag of copper scraps that Kevin had left on the bed.

From the toolbox, she removed the loom that she normally used for beading and began braiding and winding the copper wire around thin pieces of cord. When all of the wire was used, she took the thicker strips of copper and bent them into cuffs, using a clasp to attach the ends. She held one up to admire her work, and was glad to see that it was a far cry from the strands of speaker wire Zack had forced them to wear. She made the last two wristbands large enough to fit their dads, hoping it would be enough to get them home.

The clothes were the last things that needed to be put together. Carly went out to the guesthouse and carried the clothes that were in the closet into the living room, helping one boy at a time.

"We have to look as authentic as possible," she told them. "Like the people we saw in Washington, DC."

Kevin already dressed like he was from the '50s. He usually wore short-sleeve, plaid shirts, but his jeans were faded, so she noted that pants and shoes were all Kevin needed.

She tried to combine Ben's clothes to create a 1950s appearance, but everything he had brought from their house was black. She wrote in her notebook: one white short-sleeve shirt and shoes for Ben.

Zack was next. He had brought out a white T-shirt, a pair of khaki pants, and faded jeans with a hole in the knee.

"Did you not see what people were wearing?" Carly questioned. "I can't use any of this." She picked up the jeans. "This can't be all you have."

Zack leaned over and grabbed the jeans out of her hands.

"Yes, that's all I have,' he said, mocking her voice. "You know..." He paused. "I liked you better as Debbie Downer than Carly Control Freak."

Carly shot him a dirty look and continued. "Of course, you will have to do something with that hair."

"What's wrong with my hair?" he asked, running his hand through his blond hair.

"Well, besides combing it, you'll all need to use something to keep your hair under control. I didn't see one person with messy hair."

"What about you?" Zack asked in a smart-aleck tone.

"I need shoes and maybe a skirt," she said. "The vintage clothing store, Hula Hoop, next to Plug Electronics, may have what we're looking for."

"Yeah, and what about that Halloween store that's open year-round?" Kevin added.

"I always wondered who would need a costume when it wasn't Halloween. I guess now I know," Ben said.

++++++++++

Zack

Zack went into the house to tell Sharon where they were going. "Mom," he yelled, walking from room to room. He found her lying on the bed, looking ill.

"Mom, are you okay?"

"I'm fine honey, what do you need?" Sharon said softly.

"Carly wants to go to Hula Hoop, so we're going with her," Zack said.

"Let me know when you get back," she told him.

Zack could see that she was definitely not fine. He wished he could tell her that his dad had sent him The Lincoln to offer her some hope, but knew it would only make things more difficult for them. She barely let them go to the electronics store the other day. He didn't think she would be ready to let them go off time traveling.

They rode their bikes to Hula Hoop and found a salesperson who directed them to items that could be worn in the '50s. After everything was rung up, Ben paid the bill, and Kevin and Zack carried the bags out of the store. Carly smiled as she crossed the last thing off her list. *Now everything is ready for tomorrow.*

PART TWO

CHAPTER THIRTEEN

TONIGHT'S THE NIGHT

Zack

Ben, Carly, Zack, and Kevin rushed through dinner before returning to the guesthouse. Kevin pulled the chair out in front of his computer, while Ben and Zack went back to the maps. Carly picked up her notebook and the journal and sat on the couch.

"Have you been able to decode anything else?" Ben asked.

"Not yet," Carly replied. "Every time I'm on to something, it doesn't work out."

"At least you figured out Mr. Thomas and the Library of Congress," Kevin said. "If we didn't have that, we wouldn't know where to start looking."

"Yeah, tonight when we get to DC, we have to find Mr. Thomas and see what he knows," Zack said.

"What if he knows too much?" Ben said.

"Meaning?" Zack asked.

"What if he had something to do with the kidnapping?"

"I didn't think of that," Zack said. "Okay, from now on, everyone is a suspect."

"They warned us, you know," Carly said.

"What are you talking about?" Zack asked.

"It's the first thing written in the journal. 'TRUST NO ONE,'" Carly quoted.

Zack's confidence about them being able to quickly find their dads was starting to wane. "Hey twerp, make sure you get us to the library this time," he told Kevin.

"I think I know why we didn't land in the right place," Kevin said. "The first time I looked up the address for the Library of Congress, the search showed the address for the James Madison Memorial Building, which didn't exist in 1956. This time, I'm going to use the address of the Thomas Jefferson Building."

"What about the lady's voice that announces our arrival?" Zack asked.

"I took care of it," Kevin replied with his eyes on his computer monitor.

"Where are we taking off from? We sure can't do it from in here again," Ben said.

"We'd better not do it around any houses either, or someone might see us," Carly advised.

"Let's use the trail. No one will be able to see us from there," Zack said.

"Yeah," Kevin agreed, looking at the time. "We need to get ready."

Carly went to the bedroom to change her clothes. She pulled her cardigan on over her head and reached behind her to fasten the top buttons before stepping into a full skirt that fell below her knees. She carried her shoes and socks into the living room, where she sat on the couch, methodically folding each white sock down three times before tying the laces of her black-and-white saddle shoes. Zack stood in the doorway watching her.

"What in the world are you doing?"

"They used to call them triple roll socks," she answered. "It's the way they wore their socks back then."

"Why do you have your sweater on backwards?" he asked.

"Just mind your own business and go get changed," she told him.

Ben and Kevin entered the living room wearing short-sleeve shirts, white Converse sneakers, and cuffed dark-denim jeans.

"You guys look perfect, just like you stepped out of the '50s," she said, smoothing her hair and tying a colorful scarf around her ponytail.

"You look great, Sis," Ben remarked.

"Do I look like Sandy, from *Grease?*" she asked, admiring herself in the mirror.

"Kind of, except for your dark hair."

"Who's Sandy?" Kevin questioned.

"She's from some movie that Carly tortured me with one entire summer," Ben told him, making a face at Carly.

"It wasn't torture, you liked it." She twirled around, making a dance move toward him.

"You're delusional if you think I liked being forced into singing and dancing with you!" he told her. "Notice that was the last time that ever happened."

"Yeah, I noticed, spoilsport," she said with a smile.

Zack entered the room, bending and straightening his legs in an attempt to break in the stiff fabric of his jeans. He looked at Ben and Kevin, and then at Carly. "Why do you get to wear something decent and we look like dorks?" Zack asked.

"That would be because you *are* dorks," she replied. Kevin

smirked and looked away before Zack caught him.

Zack grabbed the old canvas backpack that he had found in the back of his closet and emptied the remnants of sixth grade into the trash.

"That'll work," Carly said, having determined no one carried a backpack in the 1950s. It was a smaller version that, when held by the straps, looked like a shopping bag. She took out the wristbands she had made and passed them out

"Where did you get these?" Zack asked.

"You told me that if I didn't want to wear speaker wire tied around my wrist to come up with something better. I would say these are better."

Zack examined the copper cuffs. "I have to hand it to you. These are good."

"Yeah," Ben agreed, securing his on his wrist.

"Put these in your backpack," Carly said, handing Zack the two remaining bracelets.

"What are these for?"

"They're for our dads when we find them," she replied.

"Good thinking," Zack said.

"I can't believe you were able to make these from the scraps I gave you," Kevin said.

Carly half smiled at him as she fastened the clasp on hers.

"Okay, I think we're ready," Zack said. "We can only be gone for a couple of hours; any longer than that is too risky. Kevin, you keep an eye on the time. Whatever happens, we can't get separated. There's only one coin and we're not leaving anyone behind."

Ben was the last one out of the guesthouse. He made sure they had left a light on in the living room before quietly closing the door behind him. They slipped through the opened gate and headed for the trail leading to Topanga Canyon. The wooded opening to the trail offered the seclusion they needed for Kevin to program the GPS. He wanted to avoid the rainstorm they experienced the first time they used the GPS. Since there were no Sunday entries in the journals, he skipped May 13, and entered 10:00 a.m., May 14, 1956, 10 First Street SE, Washington, DC into the device.

Their eyes nervously darted around as Kevin finished. He held out the GPS, and they each placed one hand on the handle while shifting their weight, anxious for what was to come.

"Ready?" Zack asked. With everyone's approval, Kevin pushed the button.

They winced as a painful ringing filled their ears, and the vibration of the GPS caused their bodies to tremble. Walls sprung up from the churning purple line that formed around them as they began spinning. Within seconds, they fell to the ground and, once again, found themselves surrounded by large pine trees near the Lincoln Memorial. Kevin removed the coin from the device and handed it to Zack.

+++++++++++

Carly

"Why are we here again?" Kevin asked, double-checking the screen on the device.

"Hey nitwit, I thought you had it figured out," Zack said.

"I don't know what the problem is, but I brought a map just in case this happened," Kevin replied. "The Library of Congress is straight down Independence Street, only a couple miles from here."

They followed the walkway leading to a parking lot, where they saw several taxicabs lined up along the curb.

"Hey," Ben said, pointing at the cabs. "Let's take one of those to the library. It'll save us a bunch of time."

They approached the cab at the front of the line and climbed into the back seat. Carly felt around for a seat belt, but there wasn't one.

"Thomas Jefferson Building, please," Zack stated.

"I don't drive kids without seeing the money first. That will cost you seventy-five cents," the taxi driver grumbled.

Ben pulled a dollar out his wallet. "We need to get there fast," he said, handing the driver a dollar.

The cab driver took the money, shifted the gear into drive, and floored it. Their heads snapped back and hit the seat behind them. He made a hard left at the corner, and they all slid across the seat, landing on top of Ben. The driver continued to speed down the street, then turned again, throwing them to the other side of the cab. He slammed on the brakes and they slid onto the floor, banging their heads on the back of the front seat.

The cab driver turned to them and smirked. "Thomas Jefferson Building."

"I will never tell a cab driver we're in a hurry again!" Ben said, slamming the door.

The taxi sped away, leaving them at the curb smoothing their hair and straightening their clothes.

"Whoa," Ben said, turning and facing the library.

"I thought you'd been here before," Zack said.

"No, this was the one place my mom wanted to go that we didn't get to," Ben replied, taking in the enormity of the place.

There were countless steps leading to the entrance. At the base of the stairs was a fountain featuring bronze sculptures.

"I studied the maps of the inside of this building on their website," Kevin said. He pointed to the landing at the top of the first set of stairs. "I think the main information desk is up there, through what they call the carriage entrance. I don't know if it was set up like that in 1956. We'll have to check it out."

They walked slowly by the fountain, studying the lifelike sculptures of King Neptune and his court. Ducks floated in the water among the bronze turtles and frogs. As they approached one of the nude women figures riding a seahorse, both Ben and Zack stopped in their tracks. Their eyes widened, and they looked at each other with their eyebrows lifted. Kevin saw them and giggled.

"It's art, you idiots. Keep walking," Carly said, as she pushed Ben from behind.

Carly slowly climbed the stairs, taking in the intricate carvings on the building.

"Look." She pointed at the windows on the first floor, which had detailed carvings of men's faces above them. "And there," she added. Over the front entrance were busts of nine different men, each in front of a round window. "There's Benjamin Franklin."

"This place is freaky," Zack commented. "Everywhere you look, there's a stone face staring at you."

They continued up the stairs and entered the library through the carriage entrance, trying not to look nervous as they approached the information desk. The woman behind the desk wore her hair swept up with curls meticulously arranged across the top. Pearl earrings surrounded by clear stones dangled from her ears, matching the necklace that hung from her neck. The woman's eyes were fixed on a document she was holding.

"We would like to see Mr. Thomas." Zack's voice cracked as he said the name.

The woman peered over her cat eye-shaped glasses without moving her head.

Carly examined the woman's necklace, and remembered seeing similar jewelry at the vintage store.

"Who may I say is making this request?" the receptionist asked, her cold eyes evaluating each of them.

"Lincoln, I mean the Lincolns, I mean we are all Lincolns," Zack babbled, rubbing the back of his neck.

Carly spoke up. "We're the Lincoln family and we would like to see Mr. Thomas. Do you know if he is in today, or do we need to make an appointment?"

"I'll see if he is available," the receptionist said, standing up and walking through the door behind her.

"Why did you butt in?" Zack questioned.

"Because you weren't making any sense," Carly answered.

"I was doing just fine," he defended. Ben elbowed Zack as the receptionist returned.

"Follow me," the woman instructed.

She escorted them to an office where they were advised to be seated and wait for Mr. Thomas. The room was filled with wood furniture embellished with ornate detailing. The walls were lined with bookshelves packed with books, and an American flag stood next to a high-back leather chair that sat behind a large desk. The absence of any personal items or clutter gave the impression that no one actually worked in this office.

Ben and Zack went straight for the two chairs directly across from the desk, while Kevin and Carly sat down at an adjacent table.

"Remember to watch what you say," Zack told the others.

"And how you say it," Carly added.

After a few minutes, a large older gentleman with a full head of gray hair entered the room. His white beard did not hide the scar under his ear that extended to his throat. Carly tried not to stare as she wondered what could have inflicted such a wound.

CHAPTER FOURTEEN

MR. THOMAS

Zack

"Well, well, well. What do we have here?" the man said as he sat down behind the desk.

"We're looking for—" Carly began, but Zack loudly cleared his throat and eyed her not to continue.

"Are you Mr. Thomas?" Zack asked.

"I have been called that name from time to time," the man said as the corners of his mouth turned up.

"I'm Zack Marshall and this is my brother Kevin," he said, nodding toward Kevin. "This is Ben and Carly Romano." He pointed in their direction. "We'd like to ask if you know our dads, Bill Marshall and Sam Romano?"

"Yes, I knew them well," he answered. "It saddens me to be learning of their death."

His words stunned them for only a second before they jumped out of their seats and began asking questions.

"Their death?" Kevin shouted.

"What happened to them?" Zack yelled.

"They can't be dead!" Carly practically screamed as she moved forward.

Ben climbed half on top of the desk and was inches from the man's face. "Where are they?" he growled.

By the look on Mr. Thomas's face, he didn't take kindly to Ben's actions.

"Be seated," he commanded, staring into Ben's eyes. Ben removed himself from the desk and stepped back.

Zack refused to sit down. He wasn't about to take orders from someone who may be involved in their dad's abduction. He stood with Kevin, Ben, and Carly at his side, and waited for the man to answer their questions.

"I see the apple doesn't fall far from the tree. The four of you are just as fiery as your fathers." The corners of his mouth turned up again. "Please, be seated," he said, motioning toward the chairs.

Carly and Kevin followed Zack and Ben's lead and remained standing.

"Allow me to apologize. I assumed Bill gave you the coin and he or Sam told you to come here. Something they would have done only from death's door." Mr. Thomas's gaze scanned the four of them and stopped at Ben, glaring into his eyes. "But apparently I've drawn the wrong conclusion. So, to answer your questions, I have no idea where your fathers are," he stated, and then addressed Zack. "If they are alive, why are you here?"

Zack considered how to answer Mr. Thomas's question. He glanced at the others, and they each nodded for him to go ahead.

"Five days ago, two men forced our dads into their van and drove off. We haven't seen or heard from them since," Zack informed him.

"Is that so?" Mr. Thomas said with a tone of surprise. "How do you know they are still alive?"

"They just have to be," Carly blurted out before anyone else could answer.

Mr. Thomas nodded in Carly's direction, then looked at Zack. "How did you get the coin?"

"We don't really know how it came to us. We just sort of found it," Zack informed him, not wanting to say more than the man needed to know.

They saw Mr. Thomas's eyebrow twitch.

"Bill and Sam had assured me that they had not revealed the true qualities of The Lincoln to anyone, but it's quite obvious that they passed their knowledge on to you," he said.

"No, they didn't. We figured out how to use it on our own," Kevin said proudly.

Zack recalled his dad standing at the birthday party with his pocket watch in hand, asking him if he wanted to know what was so special about The Lincoln. Zack closed his eyes. *Why didn't I just say yes!*

"You are unaware of their mission?" Mr. Thomas asked.

"What mission?" Ben questioned, still staring at the man.

Mr. Thomas nodded. "I'll get to that in a moment. First, I should tell you about the twelve coins." He eyed the empty seats. "You'll definitely want to sit down for this."

The four of them reluctantly returned to their seats and waited for him to continue.

"There was a time when our government feared for the safety of our country," Mr. Thomas said.

"They still do," Zack commented.

The man raised his hand to avoid being interrupted again. "We were in the middle of World War II when the president learned that a nuclear attack was being planned against the United States, which triggered a race to build a nuclear bomb."

"I did a paper on that. It was called the Manhattan Project," Kevin said.

"That's right," Mr. Thomas responded. "But our government wanted more than a nuclear weapon—they wanted protection. There had been a stir in the physics community about advancements that were being made in discovering a means of time travel. Meetings were arranged with the scientist who had developed the technology, and he was convinced to hand his work over to the government for the safety of the United States. A group of this country's top minds were then assembled to see if his accomplishments could be taken to the next level.

"Everyone in the group believed it was possible to create and contain the energy that would allow them to use time travel to reverse the catastrophic effect of a nuclear attack. Of course, life could not be restored to those lost during an attack, but the long-lasting effects that promised to devastate the United States would be remedied." He paused before continuing. "After months of collaboration, they decided pennies should be the vessels to contain the energy, so that the copper could be used as a conductor. One coin was made to represent each member of the group, along with a twelfth coin, designed to be the master coin."

"The Lincoln?" Carly guessed.

Mr. Thomas nodded. "Yes, The Lincoln is the twelfth coin," he said. "The twelfth coin could be used for time travel on its own, but to take the earth back in time would require the energy from all of the coins to work as one. A tablet was designed for each coin in succession to power the next, leading up to the twelfth coin."

"Where are the other eleven coins?" Ben asked.

"That's a problem your fathers have been trying to solve for most of their lives," Mr. Thomas said as he stood up and walked to the window. "When the coins were completed, they were handed over to the president, who kept them in the White House close at hand, and that's where they remained through two administrations. The problem arose when President Eisenhower had the coins moved to the Library of Congress. While the coins were being transported to the library, the courier was ambushed and his delivery truck was taken. Only a handful of people knew about the coins, so the coins couldn't have been the target. Instead, it is believed that the thieves were after a box intended for the Senate that was also in the delivery truck."

"What happened to the coins?" Carly asked.

"The thief had no idea what he truly possessed. But with all 1943 pennies having been made of steel, the coins in the tablet must have appeared to be rare 1943 copper pennies. Over time, they were sold individually to collectors around the world," Mr. Thomas said, returning to his seat. "Your grandfather gained possession of the master coin as a collector. He told me it communicated something to him that lead him to me. That's when your family's quest to reunite the twelve coins began. After your grandfather's passing, your father included Sam Romano, and together they agreed to continue the mission."

Dad's story about Grandpa giving him the pocket watch doesn't come close to this, Zack thought.

"Allowing the twelfth coin to stay in your family's possession was the agreed-upon compensation as long as the search for the coins continued." Mr. Thomas's eyes went from Zack to Ben. "If I had to guess, the first time they traveled to this office, they were about the age that you are now."

"Our dads have been trying to find the coins for that long?" Ben asked in disbelief.

"Yes, and they have achieved much success. Eight coins have been returned, along with the tablet," he said, looking at each of them.

"You possess the master coin, leaving only three coins that remain unaccounted for. It's those last three that have proven to be most elusive." He paused. "I am willing to bet that whoever is holding your fathers has possession of at least one of those coins. It's for this reason that I believe the four of you must begin your own quest to find the coins."

"I don't want to search for your coins. I just want to find our dads," Carly snapped.

"Yeah," Ben said. "All we want is to bring our dads home."

"I'm sorry you feel that way, because it appears that you don't have a choice. There are very few people who know these coins exist. I am certain the reason that someone has gone after your fathers is because they want the twelfth coin and the knowledge of how to use it. Even you, who have been able to utilize the main function of the coin, are doing so without the complete understanding of it. Since your fathers are the only ones who possess that knowledge, they should be kept alive, but without the coin in their possession, they will be in serious danger."

"Why would someone want the other coins if their only power is to support the twelfth coin?" Ben asked.

"Individually, the eleven coins are not capable of time travel, but they do have great power. The true extent of their energy cannot be tapped into unless the twelfth coin is present. Which is precisely the reason that when whoever is holding your fathers becomes aware that you have the twelfth coin, they will come after you."

Zack exchanged a worried glance with the others. *It just keeps getting worse.*

"When and where were the coins stolen?" Zack finally asked.

"The coins were taken on June 22, 1954, in Georgetown, on the corner of Wisconsin Northwest and North Street Northwest," Mr. Thomas informed them. "The robbery took place at approximately

8:45 a.m. The thief drove away in the delivery truck, and the crime remains unsolved."

"Are the eight coins that were found stored here in the library?" Ben asked.

"Yes, the tablet, along with each coin that has been recovered, is stored in a high-security area of the library," Mr. Thomas assured them.

Kevin was apprehensive about asking a question, but felt he needed to know. "The device we're using to direct the energy of The Lincoln is equipped to be precise. Do you know why we haven't been able to reach the destinations that I've programmed?"

Mr. Thomas smiled. "You are traveling by means of wormholes. Your father once described it as the difference between taking a taxi and taking a bus. The taxi takes you to the address you request, and the bus, much like the wormhole, drops you off in the general vicinity. After that you are on your own."

Kevin nodded.

"You should be aware that wormholes are ever changing and may close altogether or drop you in unexpected places. Be prepared, because an incident resulting in death is permanent."

"Did our mother know about this?" Carly asked.

"Yes," Mr. Thomas replied. "Mr. Marshall and Mr. Romano are both honorable men. They agreed there was no place for deception in a marriage."

"Apparently, it's okay to deceive the rest of the family," Ben retorted.

A beeping sound came from an intercom on top of the desk. Everyone looked at the small box, expecting someone to speak, but no voice followed. Mr. Thomas suddenly got to his feet.

"You must seek out the missing coins and observe everyone you come in contact with during your travels. Anyone who knows of the coins could be holding your fathers against their will. I wish you good luck."

The four of them stood up.

"There is one more thing," he added as he showed them to the door. "If you do recover any of the coins, which I believe it's imperative that you do, you must return them to the Library of Congress in your present time. Ask to see Mr. Jefferson. That's the name used to ensure my successor will know the nature of your visit. You should familiarize yourselves with the rules of time travel. Your fathers have told me they have been well-documented. I believe that is all I can offer you," he said, herding them out of the office door.

"Can we come back if we need your help?" Kevin asked.

"I will no longer be holding this position. I'm glad to say today is my last day. However, if I'm in the building when you visit, I will gladly meet with you. Have a safe journey home and remember, when you find the coins, you will find your fathers." He closed the door behind them.

"Boy," Ben said, moving away from the door. "He sure rushed us out of there."

"It was like he wanted to get rid of us," Zack agreed. "My dad has told the story about the copper pennies countless times, but he obviously left out the important parts."

"I think it's interesting that he said our mothers knew what was going on," Carly said as they walked down the hall. "That's why your mom isn't out publicizing the kidnappings more. She knows our dads were taken by those men because of the coins, and the police aren't going to be able to do anything about it."

"Maybe we should tell her that we have The Lincoln," Kevin said. "She might know what to do."

"If she knew what to do, she would already be doing it," Zack stated. "There's no way I'm handing The Lincoln over to Mom and watching her just sit on it while she hopes and waits for Dad and Sam to make it home on their own."

"I don't know how he did it, but your dad sent us The Lincoln. If he wanted your mom to have it, he would have sent it to her," Ben said.

"She's going to know something's up if she goes to the guesthouse and we're not there," Kevin said, having pulled the GPS out of the backpack to see the time. "We've been here for over two hours. We've got to get home."

"I told you to keep track of the time," Zack said.

"I can't help it. The magnetic field keeps screwing up my watch," Kevin replied, sliding the GPS back into the bag.

"We need to get outside," Carly said.

Finding a place to depart unnoticed proved to be a challenge. They walked a couple of blocks down the street only to settle for crouching behind some hedges. Zack pulled out the GPS and placed The Lincoln inside. He handed it to Kevin, who programmed the return time, date, and place. They each put one hand securely on the handle and Zack pushed the button.

A screeching high-pitched sound filled their ears as they watched the dome spring up from the churning purple line. Zack felt his teeth vibrating as the GPS rumbled. Within seconds they fell to the ground.

CHAPTER FIFTEEN

NO BIG DEAL

Carly

They fought the trees and bushes for a place to stand amongst the dense foliage. It was 9:00 p.m., and having gone from broad daylight instantly into darkness was disorienting. They heard the passing cars and knew they had safely made it to Topanga Canyon.

"We really need to work on reentry," Ben said, feeling a tear in his pants as he rubbed the knee he had landed on.

They brushed off their clothes and made their way across the winding street, following the path that led home.

"If we're going to land on Topanga every time we come back, we should ride our bikes up here next time so we don't have to walk home," Ben said.

Carly shook her head. "No way, there's too many branches and rocks on this trail," she said as they moved quickly down the hill.

"Well, it would be faster than this, so we'd better make it work," he replied.

The tree limb that had created so much trouble for Carly was still lying across the path. *Stupid branch*, she thought, giving it a kick. She looked down at the scab on her leg caused by her last encounter with that branch and shook her head.

"We should definitely get this out of the way," Ben said. He lined up on one side of the tree limb with the others, and they rocked it back and forth until they could roll it off to the side.

Finally, with the cul-de-sac in sight, they broke into a run. When the Marshall house came into view, it was obvious they had a problem. Every window visible from the street was illuminated. This was unusual, as Sharon always insisted that lights be turned off when not in use. They decided to enter the house through the front door instead of sneaking in the back.

Apprehensive of what was in store for them, they slowly walked up the driveway. Given the option, they would much prefer not to go in at all. Zack opened the door, and as they entered, Sharon came rushing toward them, crying hysterically and hugging each one wildly.

"Thank God, you're all right!" she bawled.

"Mom, what are you doing?" Zack asked, pulling away from her.

His mother's mood turned on a dime. She suddenly became furious.

"Where have you been? I went out to the guesthouse and you weren't there. I was just about to call the police."

"Calm down," Zack told her. "We just walked over to Ben's. Carly wanted to get some girl stuff and we wouldn't let her go alone. Of course, tagalong had to come with us." He tried to sound relaxed and as usual, irritated with his brother.

"Why didn't you tell me where you were going?"

"I don't know," Zack replied. "It didn't seem like a big deal. We weren't gone very long."

"I'm sorry," Carly said. "I didn't mean to cause any trouble."

With that, Sharon's shoulders dropped and she breathed a little deeper. "You're not in any trouble," she said. "It's just under the circumstances, I want to know when you leave the house."

"I understand," Carly replied.

"Yeah, sorry, Mom," Zack said.

"Yes," she corrected. "Why are you dressed that way she asked, stepping back to examine their clothing.

"We're having a '50s day at school next week and this is what Carly is trying to get us to wear," Zack informed her.

"Well, you've done a great job, Carly. You guys definitely look like you're from the '50s." Sharon wiped her nose with a tissue. "I think we've all had enough for one night, so off to bed, and don't leave this house again without telling me," she warned.

"Okay, Mom," Kevin said.

"Oh, Carly, here, I forgot to give this to you earlier. I picked it up this morning." Sharon reached into the drawer of the small table in the entryway and handed Carly her phone.

"Awesome! Thank you so much!" Carly exclaimed.

When Carly got to her room, she grabbed the charger from her bag and plugged in her phone. It took a few minutes before she was able to send Zack a text.

"Don't keep blaming everything on me, and I'm not kidding!"

+++++++++

Kevin and Carly went to the guesthouse early the next morning. Kevin headed straight to his computer. Carly lingered in the doorway and could see Zack and Ben sitting in the leather chairs opposite one another.

"Ben, come out here for a minute," she said.

Ben slowly got out of the chair and went outside. "What's up?"

"It's your ex-girlfriend," she replied.

He squinted his eyes, looking at her. "What?" he asked with irritation.

"It's Francesca, she's blowing up my phone," Carly said, turning around her phone so he could see the list of unanswered texts. "She says you left a message for her to call you, and she's trying to get ahold of you, but you're not answering."

Ben walked toward the pool.

"Is that true?" Carly asked, following him. "I mean, I couldn't care less if you called her, just call her back already so she'll stop texting me."

"I called her before Dad and Bill were kidnapped," he admitted. "When we booked the gig at the school dance, I planned on asking Frankie to go with me, but before I had the chance to talk to her, all this stuff happened with Dad." He sat down on the end of a lounge chair and put his head down.

"You can't just not call her back," Carly said.

"Really?" Ben said with attitude, lifting his chin. "And what am I supposed to say? Think about it: first I break up with her 'cause Mom was sick. Now, just when I was going to ask if she wanted to hang out, Dad disappears. What are we, some freakazoid family that terrible things keep happening to? How would I explain our most recent drama? Our dad is missing, and by the way, I won't be able to spend much time with you because I have to search for these lost coins so that we can find him. Oh, and did I mention that we're time traveling? You believe me, don't you?" Ben shook his head. "It even sounds ridiculous to me, and I'm living it! I'm definitely not calling her back!"

"Okay, I'll do it," she said, waving her phone in the air. "What do you want me to tell her?"

"I'm not asking you to call her for me!" he yelled. "If you want to call her, do it on your own. Do whatever you want, I don't care, just don't bring her name up to me again."

Carly's eyebrows rose as he stormed back into the guesthouse. She stayed outside for a few minutes before following him in and flopping down on the couch. Ben had returned to the chair across from Zack, and Kevin was still in front of the computer. These had become their workstations.

"If you guys can think of anything that might help me break the code in the journal, I'm open to suggestions," Carly said, hoping Ben was still speaking to her. "Kevin emailed me the last page and I've been working on it every night before I fall asleep, but I haven't been able to find a match for whatever code they used."

"There has to be something online that can help, just keep looking," Zack told her, handing her Kevin's tablet.

"All right." She sighed, hoping that one of the others would volunteer to relieve her of this responsibility, but no such luck. She got up and took a small pad of paper from the pile on the bookshelf.

Zack looked at Carly. "Mr. Thomas laid a lot on us yesterday, and before we make any decisions about what we're going to do next, we should gather as much information as we can. Kevin, you look up wormholes, Ben's on the coins, and I'm working on the rules of time travel. That leaves the theft of the coins. See if you can find something on crimes in DC around that date."

Carly began her search and made some notes on her findings while the others appeared to be doing the same, and after a while, her eyes drifted out of the window. "What I don't understand is how they could've done it," she said. "Our dads have always been there for us. When would they have had time to recover all of those coins?"

"I was wondering the same thing," Kevin said.

"They must have done it while they were at work," Zack commented, looking up from his laptop.

"I don't think it was while they were at work," Ben said. "I think it's when they were supposedly playing…" At the same moment, they all four looked at each other and said, "Golf."

"We need to talk to Jim," Ben continued. "He's been the pro at Calabasas Country Club for as long as I can remember. He'll know if something was going on. Today's Saturday so he should be there."

CHAPTER SIXTEEN

THE PRO

Carly

The sound of Sharon entering the guesthouse drew their attention. Carly took one look at the dark circles under Sharon's eyes and quickly hid behind her tablet so as to not reveal her stunned expression. Sharon's hair, which was usually perfect, was disheveled, and she was still wearing her robe. Carly eyed Ben, and the surprised look on his face told her he was thinking the same. They had been so freaked out about getting caught the night before, they hadn't noticed the drastic change in Sharon's appearance.

"What are you guys doing?" Sharon asked, glancing around the room.

"You mentioned school last night, so we thought we had better go over our homework assignments," Zack said.

"That's great," she muttered. "Why is all of your gaming stuff put away?"

Carly saw the blank look on Sharon's face as she scanned the room.

"The TV is broken," Zack answered.

"What's the matter with it?" Sharon asked, moving toward the television.

Kevin's eyes got big and he took in a sharp breath.

Zack wadded up a piece of paper and whipped it at Kevin's head. "Don't say a word," Zack mouthed to Kevin.

Sharon didn't notice Zack's warning to Kevin. She was busy pushing the on/off button to the television. Her eyes followed the cord into the wall. "When did this happen?"

"The other day, it just stopped working and we didn't want to bother you with it." Zack then quickly changed the subject. "May we go to the club for lunch?"

"Yes," she replied, distracted as she continued to look around the room.

"Oh, Mom, I wanted to ask you," Zack said. "Some of the guys are bugging us to go see a movie and get sushi tomorrow. They heard about Dad and I think it's their way of trying to take our minds off things for a while."

"What about your baseball game? Oh no!" Sharon exclaimed. "I just remembered you never brought your sports bag home from the Romanos' so I could wash your uniform." She breathed in deeply as her trembling hand covered her mouth.

Carly felt sick as she watched Sharon's image of perfection crumble right before their eyes.

"No worries, Mom. I was going to call the coach, but I forgot. There's no way I can play baseball right now."

She sighed with relief. "Of course," she said. "I'll call him for you."

"So, what do you think about tomorrow?" Zack asked.

"What about tomorrow?" She sounded distracted.

"The movies. Mom, are you okay?"

"Yes. Of course, the movies," she said, blinking her eyes as if she was struggling to focus. "You've been cooped up back here for the entire week. I think you should go. Let me know when you leave for the club." She walked out of the guesthouse and closed the door behind her.

"I don't care what she says, she's not okay!" Kevin said.

"You're right," Carly said, turning to Zack. "And you were able to keep a straight face while you sat there and told lie after lie." She shook her head. "It's really disturbing to watch someone be so deceitful. I guess we're lucky to have someone on our side who can look his mother in the eye and tell a bold-faced lie."

"Yes, you are lucky, Little Miss Negative," Zack said, leaning back in his chair, folding his hands behind his head. "I just paved our way for travel tomorrow."

"Knock it off, you two," Ben warned.

Carly rolled her eyes and picked up her phone.

"Let's go to the club. Bring your notes; we can go over them while we're there," Zack said. "I'll go tell Mom we're leaving."

++++++++++

It was more than two miles to the club and they knew the streets that would get them through the hills the fastest. The iron gate of the ranch-style clubhouse nestled in the mountains was open when they arrived. The guard waved them in and they raced across the parking lot. Carly, Ben and Kevin slowed as they approached the bike rack, but Zack whizzed past.

"You might want to read the sign," Carly yelled. Zack ignored her as he turned the corner, descending down the hill. "He never follows the rules," she mumbled, staring at the posted sign that read "Golf

Carts Only Beyond This Point".

"Come on," Ben waved to her. He and Kevin were already running down to the lower level. "I bet Jim knows something. We should have come here sooner."

Carly caught up with them as they entered the pro-shop.

"Is Jim around?" Ben asked the man behind the counter.

"Yes, he should be back any minute."

"Thanks," Ben replied. "We'll wait."

Carly slowly walked around looking at all the golf equipment for sale, remembering the countless times she had been there with her dad.

The door opened and Jim entered followed by a young man. "Book his next lesson," Jim told the man behind the counter.

The young man pulled out his phone ready to input the time.

"Get back to the range when you're through here," Jim told him. "Try to get a feel for what we worked on today and I'll see you next week."

"Okay Jim, thanks," the young man said.

"Whose bike is that out there?" Jim asked, annoyed.

The man behind the counter pointed in Zack's direction. "These kids are here for you."

"Hey you guys, good to see you?" Jim removed his hat. "Any news about your fathers?"

"No, nothing."

"I knew you would want to talk to me," Jim said. "It was only a matter of time."

"You were expecting us?" Carly asked.

"Of course, if my dad was missing, you'd better believe I would be tracing his last steps," Jim replied.

"Were you here when they played Monday?" Ben asked.

"Yes, and I'll tell you the same thing I told the police." Jim's eyes went to the door as two women walked in. "Let's go outside." He moved toward the door and they followed.

Once outside Jim stepped away from the building and stopped, the others leaned in, anxious to hear what he was about to say. "Your dads only played the front nine Monday, then asked for their clubs to be cleaned and loaded into their car. They bought a couple boxes of balls and went upstairs. It was some time before I noticed they had left the balls on the counter so I ran out to try to catch them. That's when I saw that they were parked in front of the clubhouse talking with two men. I didn't think anything of it till I got close and overheard some of what they were saying."

"Were the men members?" Zack questioned.

"I'd never seen them before," Jim replied.

"What did you hear them say?" Carly asked.

"They told your dads that they'd better be *there* and have *it* with them."

"Be where? Have what?" Kevin cried.

"I don't know. After they saw me, they didn't say another word. They went over to their car, opened the back doors, and got in."

"Back doors?" Ben questioned.

"Yes, they had a driver, but the windows were tinted and I couldn't see in."

"What did the men look like?" Carly asked.

"They were on the other side of your dad's Range Rover and I couldn't see their faces, but one of them was really tall and the other one was about half his size. There was such a big difference between them that they looked strange walking next to each other."

"That's them!" Carly shouted.

"You know those guys?" Jim asked.

Zack looked at Carly and shook his head. She got the message. "No, but I've seen them before," she replied.

"When I handed your dad the balls," Jim said to Ben, "he acted kind of strange. I mean, he said thanks and everything, but something wasn't right. It was about then that their clubs were brought out and they left."

"Can you remember anything else?" Ben asked.

"Well, the whole thing seemed a little off to me, so I went over to talk to the guard. He checks in anyone who's not a member, and I wanted to see who those men were. As it turned out he had been on his lunch break and there was no one to relieve him so he had just left the gate open."

"That means there's no record of their names or license plate number, right?" Zack asked.

"That's right," Jim replied. "The police were going to take a look at the security cameras, but I don't know what came of that."

"Thanks for telling us all of this, Jim," Carly said.

"There is something else," Jim added, "but I don't know if it has anything to do with what happened Monday."

"What is it?" Kevin asked.

He took a deep breath and they waited for him to continue. "You're going to think this is crazy, but I'm just going to say it." He stopped and breathed again. "Something strange happens when your fathers play a round of golf. They go out and after they get past the stables on eleven, they disappear and I mean they really disappear. I've only seen it happen once, but I know what I saw." He paused and looked at each of them.

"Go ahead." Ben encouraged.

"The two of them were standing by a tree and all of a sudden they vanished into thin air. Scared me to death, I looked all over for them," he said, shaking his head as if he was still affected by the experience. "I thought I was losing my mind. Then a few hours later they finished their round and drove their cart up to the clubhouse like nothing happened. I've asked them about it and they've never given me a straight answer. I didn't mention this to the police because there's no proof of it, plus they probably would've rushed me to the psych ward thinking there was something wrong with me. But given the circumstances I thought you guys should know."

"Thank you," Zack told Jim.

"Yeah, that's a big help," Ben added.

Kevin and Carly said, "Thanks," and started around the corner to the snack bar.

"Hey," Jim yelled, and they looked back to see him pointing. "Get that bike out of here and I don't want to see it down here again."

"Yes, sir," Zack replied.

Carly cocked her head lifted her eyebrows giving Zack her best *I told you so* expression as he pushed his bike up the hill and quickly returned. He stood looking out across the golf course and the Santa Monica Mountains.

"Where are you guys?" Carly heard Zack whisper. He was still for a moment as if he expected for his question to be answered, then turned and took a seat.

"Let's go over this stuff before we order anything," Zack said and the others nodded. "Okay, start with the coins." He looked at Ben.

"The 1943 copper pennies," Ben began, but was interrupted. A friend of their parents stopped at their table and started asking question after question regarding their fathers' disappearance. When he finally left, they saw another one of their dad's buddies moving in their direction.

"This was a bad idea. Let's get out of here, before people start lining up," Zack said, as he got to his feet. The others followed suit and left the snack bar before anyone else could get to them.

CHAPTER SEVENTEEN

THE RULES

Zack

They pulled up, dropped their bikes on the side of the garage, and hurried to the guesthouse.

"Go tell Mom we're home," Zack told Kevin.

"Don't start without me," Kevin replied as he took off running, and was back before anyone had a chance to pull out their notes.

"Okay, what do we have?" Zack asked.

"I really didn't find anything that we didn't already know," Ben said. "There are 1943 copper pennies known to exist that people think are rare collectables. But I did turn up something interesting that happened in the 1950s."

"What's that?" Carly asked.

"A bunch of 1943 copper pennies started surfacing, but when the authorities looked into it, they found that people had taken 1948 pennies and cut part of the eight away to look like a three. Some others were steel coins that had been copper plated. It was easy to tell the fakes that were copper plated," he said as he looked up from his notes. "If the penny stuck to the magnet, it was just a steel penny with a copper coating."

"Why would people go through all that trouble to make fake pennies?" Kevin wondered out loud.

"Money," Ben told him. "Collectors pay plenty for these things. There was something else that happened, but it was in 1944."

"What?" Kevin asked.

"The 1943 steel pennies didn't work out, so the next year the government went back to using copper. But when they pressed the new 1944 copper pennies there were some steel blanks still in the machine from the year before, and those blanks became 1944 steel pennies. These coins are so valuable that someone just paid over a million dollars for one."

"Wow! A million dollars for a penny!" Kevin marveled.

"Kevin, what have you found out about wormholes?" Zack asked.

"They are actually traversable wormholes, and they allow travel from one time to another very quickly. They're areas of warped space-time that curve back onto themselves with great energy."

"Okay, what?" Zack made a face. "Warped space-time?"

"Yeah, it's energy that creates tunnels with two open ends, allowing the traveler to go from one time and space to another," Kevin informed them. "The tunnels are kept open by exotic forms of matter, like negative energy. A device releasing a stream of negative energy would ensure the tunnel would remain open for the return trip."

"I think Carly puts out enough negative energy to cover us on that," Zack commented.

Carly rolled her eyes and gestured for Kevin to continue.

"This is serious. It's a dangerous way to travel," Kevin said with concern. "If one end of the wormhole snaps shut, we won't be able to get through. We'll just be stuck out there to die."

Zack cut him off. "Is that all you've got?" he asked. Not wanting to hear more about how dangerous it was, since there really wasn't anything they could do about it.

"Isn't that enough?" Kevin replied.

"Carly, your turn," Zack moved on.

"I couldn't find anything on the actual theft of the pennies, but Mr. Thomas said something about a box that was in the delivery truck with the coins."

"Yeah, he said the box was headed for the Senate and that's what the thief was going after," Ben said.

"Right, so I looked up what was going on in the Senate the week the coins were stolen, and found that there was a subcommittee holding hearing on juvenile delinquency. People were saying kids were acting out and breaking laws because of all the violence they were seeing on TV and reading in comic books. They demanded that the government do something about it. Apparently, it was a really big deal."

"I didn't even know they had television way back in 1954." Ben pointed at the TV. "What kind of violence could they have shown back then?"

"I don't know," Carly replied. "They came down even harder on the comic book industry. But when it turned out that only a few letters from concerned citizens were presented at the hearing, it wasn't enough public support for the Senate to do anything more, so the network representatives were let off easy."

"And this is important, why?" Zack tapped his finger impatiently on the arm of his chair.

"Because if we can figure out who would benefit from that box being stolen, it might lead us to the thief."

"It would help if we knew what was in the box, because without that, the thief could be anyone involved in those hearings," Ben said.

"Which doesn't narrow it down much," Carly admitted, closing the notepad she had been reading from.

"My turn," Zack said. "There's tons of information out there on what could be the rules of time travel, and after searching through them, these are the ones that make the most sense:

1. You must be able to travel at or faster than the speed of light.
2. You cannot travel prior to the date that the technology you are using was developed.
3. A person traveling through time must not be seen by family members or anyone that may recognize them. This could cause confusion and would be dangerous for all involved.
4. An incident resulting in death to the traveler is permanent."

"Wow." Carly pushed her hair out of her face. "We should have found out all of that stuff before we ever used the GPS."

"Why? It wouldn't have changed anything." Zack stood and began pacing. "The Lincoln is stamped 1943, so we won't be able to travel to a year before that, but we shouldn't need to. I guess now we just have to make the decision. Should we become coin seekers?" He stopped and looked at the others. "I think Mr. Thomas was right. Someone wanting The Lincoln is holding our dads, and the only way we're going to find them is by getting those lost coins."

Ben nodded in agreement. "I didn't like it when Mr. Thomas said it, but he was right. We have to find the coins and return them to the Library of Congress to even have a chance of finding our fathers."

"Someone's going to come looking for us when they find out we have The Lincoln, so I think we should let the coins lead us to them first," Carly stated.

"I'm with Carly," Kevin said.

"Okay, we're all in. Now we need to figure out a travel schedule," Zack said. "We're already cleared to go tomorrow afternoon." He looked at Carly and bowed his head. "Thanks to me." She rolled her eyes and he continued. "My mom is going to be all paranoid when we go back to school Monday, so we should probably wait until Tuesday night before we go again. The dance will be our cover on Friday."

"I hope we find them on our first try." Carly looked out of the window.

"Don't get your hopes up, but we aren't going to stop looking until we do find them, I can promise you that!" Zack assured.

CHAPTER EIGHTEEN

SCENE OF THE CRIME

Carly

The plan was to leave for the movies at noon.

"What do you think?" Carly asked, modeling the clothes she chose to wear. "I think these pants will pass for pedal pushers. Don't you?"

"I have no idea what you're talking about," Ben said.

"Pedal pushers are short pants people wore in the '50s," she told him, putting on white socks and slipping her feet into her loafers.

"Then I guess they're all right," he replied.

She blew a huff of air through her nose. "Thanks for the help."

"Put our shirts and shoes in your backpack," Zack told Ben. "We'll put them on when we get to the lookout. My mom might think something's up if she catches us in these clothes again."

Kevin brought over his things and Ben stuffed their shirts and shoes into his backpack.

"I'll meet you guys by the bikes," Zack told them as he opened the door and went up to the main house.

Kevin took Zack's backpack and Ben attached his to the seat of his bike. Carly was already at the end of the driveway when Zack came running out of the side gate.

"Okay, we're cool," he said, mounting his bike. He looked at Kevin. "I told Mom that we'd be back around five thirty. So pay attention to the time, and don't screw up!"

They took off toward the trail and labored up the path. After reaching the top, they waited for a break in the heavy traffic. Finally, they were able to cross Topanga Canyon Boulevard to the lookout.

"Let's hide our bikes in here," Ben said, separating the branches of two shrubs. They shoved their bikes into the small space, dragging over a tree branch to hide their rear wheels. The boys changed their shirts and shoes, while Carly hid Ben's backpack with their bikes. Kevin had already programmed the GPS to arrive early on the morning the coins were stolen—June 22, 1954, at 8:00 a.m. They each put one hand on the GPS and Zack pushed the button.

Their eyes squinted and their shoulders rose as the piercing ringing sound penetrated their ears. Walls shot up from the churning purple line, dividing them from the outside world. They began to spin, and a moment later they found themselves on the ground, surrounded by three large pine trees near the Lincoln Memorial.

"Is this the only wormhole opening in DC?" Zack complained, removing The Lincoln from the GPS. "I would like to land closer to the address we're putting in this thing for a change."

They walked to the same parking area as they had before and approached one of the cabs. Zack opened the door and they all climbed in.

"Where to?" the cab driver asked.

"Wisconsin Northwest and North Street Northwest."

"Georgetown, huh?" the driver said as he reached outside of the car, near the side mirror and flipped the meter before pulling away from the curb.

After about ten minutes, they reached the corner that Zack requested. Ben paid the driver and they stepped out of the cab, finding themselves in a small village. The narrow sidewalks were paved with bricks, and storefronts stood just a few feet from the curb. Shops that lined the streets were mostly two- and three-story brick buildings, giving the feeling of a big city in a small town. Aside from customers frequenting the bakery, the street was relatively empty.

Carly saw the names on the street signs, and from the information Mr. Thomas had given them, knew that they were in the right place. They walked toward the corner and began surveying the area. Unsure of exactly where the theft took place, they appraised the view of the intersection from every angle, looking for a spot that would provide the best sight line. They finally selected a doorway for Ben and Carly, while Zack and Kevin stood just a few feet away near the edge of the building. They observed every car that passed as the minutes ticked closer to the moment of the crime that ultimately resulted in their dads' disappearance.

"What are you looking at?" a voice from behind them asked.

They all jumped, startled by the newcomer.

"Who are you?" Zack asked.

Carly stared at the kid who looked to be around Kevin's age and wondered if he could be the thief.

"Earl Jackson, who are you?" the boy replied.

He was a little taller than Kevin, with dark skin and freckles on his nose. His hair was cropped close to his head. Smartly dressed, he wore a crisp, white button-down shirt and black pants.

Some commotion drew their attention back to the street. Earl started to go investigate, but Zack grabbed him by the shirt and pulled him against the building, gesturing for him to be quiet.

"What are you doing? Let go of me!" Earl demanded.

Zack released his grip. "It's for your own safety. Stay here and don't make a sound," he whispered.

Zack, Kevin, and Earl peered around the corner from their vantage point. Ben and Carly also had a perfect view.

A man wearing a stocking pulled over his head was standing next to a white delivery truck at the stop sign. He pointed a gun in the driver's window, shouting for the driver to get out. As the driver opened the door, the man grabbed him and threw him to the ground, then jumped into the truck and sped away. The driver yelled at the man to stop, but the truck was out of sight within seconds.

Ben and Zack ran to the man lying in the street.

"Are you hurt?" Zack asked.

"No, I don't think so," the driver answered, rubbing his arm. "Did you see that? He drove off in my truck." The man looked around in disbelief. "I need to get to a telephone and call the police." He got to his feet and quickly moved toward the drugstore.

People from the nearby shops began coming out to see what was causing the disturbance. Zack and Ben went back across the street.

"I can't believe he got away. We're no closer than we were before," Carly whined.

Earl gave her a quizzical look. "You were all lined up here ready to watch. Did you know this was going to happen?"

"Not exactly," Ben lied.

"I have to go. I can't be late for work," Earl said, looking down the street. "My bus should be here by now."

"Sorry I grabbed you like that," Zack apologized.

"I'm glad you did," Earl said. "Otherwise I'd have been out in the open and the thief would've recognized me." He paused for a second. "If I would've kept walking, he might have thought I was sneaking up on him. I could've gotten shot."

"You said he would have recognized you. Do you know who the man is?" Ben asked.

"I suspect I do," Earl said slowly. His eyes squinted as he rephrased what he asked earlier. "You guys were hiding like you knew he was going to steal that truck."

Carly glanced from Ben to Earl. *We've got to get the name of the thief from this kid,* she thought.

"It's important for us to find out who that man with the gun was," Ben confided.

"I've got to go," Earl said. "But if you want to know more about that scoundrel, I can help you with that. I owe you at least that much." He looked down the street again and started walking. "There's my bus." The bus stopped at the corner and the door slid open. "If you want to ride with me to work, I'll tell you about him," he called back to them before getting on.

Zack grabbed his backpack, and they ran toward the bus, barely making it. Ben dug into his pocket for four dimes that would cover their fare. Commuters were scattered throughout the bus, and they found Earl seated alone with an empty bench across from him. Carly sat next to Earl, while the others took the bench.

"How could you have known who that was? His face and body were completely covered," Carly said.

"His shoes," Earl replied. "It's part of my job. Shoes tell a lot about a person." He looked down at Carly's shoes curiously. "Like the shoes you're wearing. There's something different about them."

"Are you even old enough to have a job?" Carly changed the subject as she bent her knees, sliding her feet under the seat.

"I'll be fourteen next week." Earl sat up tall and puffed out his chest.

"What kind of place would hire a thirteen-year-old?" Carly asked.

"My uncle's friend owns a barbershop near the government

buildings," he answered. "I only work Saturdays during the school year, but I'm putting in a full week now that summer's here. Our patrons are top government officials, senators, and congressmen," he bragged. "We do plenty of regular folk as well. It's my job to sweep hair, put the magazines and newspapers in their place, and shine the shoes of anyone who needs it."

Carly crinkled her nose at the idea of a kid his age having a job. Not to mention him being allowed to take a bus across town all by himself every day. *I guess things were different in 1954.*

"You know who the thief is because of his shoes?" she asked.

"Yes." Earl nodded.

"Are you going to give this information to the police?" Kevin questioned.

"They aren't going to hunt a man down 'cause I recognized his shoes. It's best if I don't get myself involved."

The bus driver announced a stop and pulled over. A few people exited the bus and the driver pulled away from the curb.

"They call him Shorty," Earl said.

"I can see why. He's not very tall," Kevin said.

"Don't let that fool you—he's trouble." Earl nodded to Kevin. "He's mixed up in all kinds of illegal activities."

"How do you know that?" Ben asked.

"It's no secret. He runs his business out of the diner a few doors down from the barbershop. His customers meet him there to set up jobs. He shows up most days around three o'clock." Earl stood and reached for the cord that ran above the windows. A bell sounded, and the driver's voice loudly announced the next stop.

"This is it," he said.

They got off the bus and walked down the block to the barbershop. A red, white, and blue striped barber pole was attached to the front of the building. The large writing on the plate glass window read "Brock's Barbershop." They stepped inside and could barely move. The shop was set up to utilize every inch of the small space. Customers were waiting in two of the three chairs that surrounded a low table covered with the morning newspapers.

"Hey, Mr. Brock," Earl said.

"Don't hey me, you're late," Mr. Brock replied.

"I'm sorry. I need to start taking an earlier bus. That eight forty-five was late again. This is my boss, Mr. Brock," Earl said, and waited for his companions to introduce themselves. They did, and said that they were visiting Washington, DC with their parents.

Mr. Brock was working on a customer, yet took the time to exchange pleasantries. "If your friends want a haircut, they are welcome to stay. Otherwise, they best get going. There's plenty of work to be done."

"Yes, sir," Earl said, grabbing a white smock from the hook in the corner and putting it on as he led them out the door. "Come back tomorrow just before three o'clock, and you might get to see Shorty for yourselves."

"Thanks, we will," Ben said.

They walked down the street and passed the store Carly had gone into on their first visit.

"Hey, the bus brought us back toward the Lincoln Memorial," Kevin pointed out, taking note of the name of the street for their return.

They ducked into the empty doorway of an office building before putting The Lincoln into the GPS. Kevin worked the toggle knob, inputting the information for their return trip, and held out the device. They each prepared themselves and put their hand on the mount.

"Ready?" Kevin asked. With everyone's approval, he pushed the button.

The ringing sound was excruciating. Within seconds, the purple line poured around them, sprouting their protection. The ground beneath their feet was gone and they were soon thrown to the ground at the lookout on Topanga Canyon. They hurried to uncover their bikes, and with a break in traffic they were home earlier than expected.

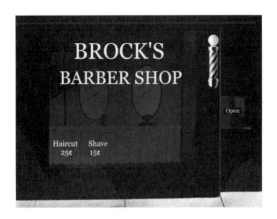

CHAPTER NINETEEN

TIME SHIFTERS

Zack

That evening, Sharon joined them in the guesthouse, seeming a little better. Kevin and Carly were sitting on opposite ends of the couch while Ben and Zack were on the leather chairs across from one another. They had thrown the maps under the couch when they heard her coming.

"Tomorrow we're back to the school week schedule." She eyed Kevin and Carly. "I've allowed you both to stay in the guesthouse until all hours of the night. Now I want you in the house by 9:00 p.m." Sharon turned to Ben. "What are your after-school activities this week?"

"I've got band rehearsal Tuesday and the dance on Friday," Ben answered.

"I'm glad you're performing at the dance," she told him. "I know your father was looking forward to it. How about you, Carly? What's your schedule?"

"All I have planned is the dance," Carly said. "But we do need to go home and get some school clothes."

"Of course, do you want me to come with you?"

"We've got it, Mom," Zack said.

"Would it be possible for me to use your washer and dryer?" Carly asked.

"I can do that for you," Sharon offered.

"I would really rather do it myself, if that's all right. It's my main chore at home."

"You're welcome to use the laundry room anytime. Let me know if there are any changes," Sharon said as she left the guesthouse.

++++++++++

After suffering a long first day back at school, the night seemed even longer. They were relieved Tuesday when the final school bell rang.

"Was yesterday the longest day ever?" Kevin asked.

"Sure seemed like it," Zack agreed. "Today didn't feel any shorter. At least we're traveling tonight."

"I know," Carly said. "We should've tried to go last night. I can't stand to think of that Shorty person knowing something about our dads and not being able to get to him. At least we only have to wait a few more hours." She had just picked up her phone to check the time when the door to the guesthouse opened.

"Hey, it's all set," Ben announced, having returned from band rehearsal. "The guys will cover for me."

"What did you tell them?" Zack asked.

"That I wasn't going to be able to play at the dance, because I have something very important to take care of," he said, falling back into the chair.

"And they were okay with that?" Zack asked, a bit surprised.

"Not really. Taylor has this producer coming to see us, and they wanted to know what could be more important than that. I told them it had to do with our dads."

"You told them that?" Carly questioned.

"Yeah, why not? It's the truth."

"It is that," Zack agreed.

"There is one catch," Ben told them.

"What?" Zack asked, afraid of what was coming next.

"I agreed to play one song with them so that we don't come off like flakes to this producer guy. They're getting someone to sub for me the rest of the set. I know it's going to cut into our time, but I couldn't just leave them hanging."

"I think it's perfect," Zack said. "We need to establish a presence there anyway. Play the first song and then we'll slip out. That'll still give us about three hours if everything goes as planned."

"You're not going to believe what they want to name the band," Ben said.

"What?" Carly asked.

"They want to call us the Time Shifters."

"You're kidding," Zack said.

"Yeah, Adam and Taylor think it's a good name because we play songs from different time periods."

"I like it," Zack said.

"I don't know, Time Shifters sounds a little too cosmic to me," Ben said.

"What do you want the name to be?" Carly asked.

"That's the problem. I can't think of anything, so it's hard to argue. Adam created artwork that goes with the name. Some of it's kind of cool. I hate always being the holdout."

He sat in the chair across from Zack and thought for a few minutes.

"I'm just going to tell them that I'm okay with it. It's better than some of the other names they've come up with." He picked up his phone and sent a text to Adam agreeing to Time Shifters as the name for their band. "So, what's our plan for tonight?" Ben asked Zack when he finished.

"We have to wait until my mom is asleep. She goes to bed late, so set your phone alarms for 2:00 a.m.," he told Carly and Kevin. "Remember to put them on vibrate just in case you fall asleep. With Dad gone, she's going to be on high alert, so be sure not to make any noise when you leave the house."

"We'll meet in front of the guesthouse."

++++++++++

Carly

Kevin and Carly waited anxiously in their rooms. Alarms weren't necessary, because no one fell asleep. At precisely 2:00 a.m., Carly stood in the backyard after sneaking out of the house per Zack's instructions. He knew she would never be able to maneuver around the squeaky spots on the stairs the way Kevin could. The room she was staying in had doors that opened onto a balcony, and Zack put a ladder up against the trellis that extended from the first floor to make it easier for her to come down.

She saw some movement in the dark and realized the boys were waiting for her by the back gate. They rode their bikes up the path, which Carly wished they had done a better job clearing. They finally made it to the lookout and pushed their bikes far into the bushes. Kevin programmed June 23, 1954, Washington, DC into the GPS, and they held on as Zack pushed the button. The sharp ringing sound was painful to their ears, and the jarring vibration rattled their bodies. They began to spin. The bubble around them dissipated as they hit the ground.

"Man, I hate this!" Ben yelled. "I feel like my head is going to burst."

"I know, me too," Carly said, blinking to adjust her eyes to the brightness, having come from the dead of night to two thirty in the afternoon.

Zack and Kevin both nodded.

The same three pine trees offered the privacy they needed to arrive unseen as they once again landed near the Lincoln Memorial. Zack removed the coin from the GPS and put it into his back pocket, while Kevin pulled out his map. The barbershop was only a few blocks away. They walked quickly to make sure they would arrive with time to spare. As they approached the barbershop, they saw Earl sweeping the sidewalk in front of the building.

"Hi, guys," Earl greeted them as they got closer.

"Hey, Earl," they all replied.

"I've been thinking about you since you left yesterday and I was wondering." Earl paused. "You said you were here visiting DC with your parents. Is your family staying at a campsite?"

Carly laughed. "What would make you think that?"

Earl pointed to Zack's backpack. "He's carrying around that knapsack which means you're either camping or hiking, but you guys don't seem like the type to do either."

"Oh, that bag?" Carly pointed to Zack's backpack. "He always carries that thing around. It's kind of like his purse." She tried to suppress a smile.

"It's not a purse," Zack defended.

"You never said where you were from," Earl commented.

"We're from Calabasas, California," Ben informed him, while Zack and Carly exchanged dirty looks.

"That explains it," Earl said, drawing Carly's attention.

"Explains what?" she asked.

"There's something different about you guys, and it must be because you're from California," he said, leaving Carly a little insulted by his comment.

"Has our thief shown up at the diner?" Ben asked.

"Not yet. He always takes the corner booth in the back. There is only one other booth back there, so try to sit there if you can. There's never anyone in the diner at this time of day, so you shouldn't have a problem. Order a malt and they'll let you sit there all day."

"Thanks. Do you want to come?"

"No, I work till five. Plus, he knows who I am. It's best if he doesn't notice you're there."

CHAPTER TWENTY

THE THIEF

Zack

The shiny black-and-white checkerboard floor was the first thing they noticed as they entered the diner, along with the man in the paper hat who was busy tending to the few customers sitting at the counter. They weaved their way through several short rows of metal tables with shiny chrome legs and red vinyl chairs. No tablecloths or place settings were laid out on the tables, only condiments serving as a centerpiece.

They continued on to one of the booths at the far end of the restaurant, as Earl suggested. Zack slid across the seat to make room for Ben, while Kevin and Carly sat across from them. Kevin dealt out the small menus he found between the napkin holder and the large, glass sugar dispenser.

"You're not getting a veggie burger here," Zack told Carly.

"No kidding," she said as she looked over the menu. "No wonder so many old people have heart problems; they grew up eating this junk," she said, putting down her menu. She picked up the glass sugar dispenser. "What on earth would you ever need this much sugar for?"

"I don't have a problem with the menu," Kevin said.

Zack watched Carly look down and scrunch her nose up at the sugar she was holding before returning it to the table and examining her empty hand.

"You are such a freak," he told her.

"Zack," Ben said with a warning.

"I need to wash my hands." Carly ignored Zack as she looked around for the restroom. "Did anyone bring any antibacterial soap?" She glanced at the three of them. The boys just looked at her as if she had two heads.

Soon, the waitress took their order and returned with a tray of burgers and fries. They ate slowly, trying to draw out the meal, but when they were finished there was still no sign of Shorty. The busboy cleared the last of the dishes, leaving only their water glasses. It had been nearly an hour since they'd arrived at the diner. They were just about to give up when a thin, wiry man carrying a large box walked in and headed for the booth next to theirs.

"Could that be him?" Kevin asked.

The man slid the box onto the seat directly behind Zack and Ben and sat down beside it.

"Will you be havin' the usual today, Shorty?" the waitress asked.

"No, I'll just have a cup of coffee and a piece of that cherry pie," Shorty replied.

"Coming right up," the waitress said.

To Carly's dismay, he lit a cigarette. "That's disgusting," she whispered, looking around. "Is he allowed to smoke in here?"

Shorty had only been there a minute when Zack became aware of an uncomfortable feeling in the seat of his pants. There was a low, rumbling vibration coming from The Lincoln in his back pocket, which felt oddly similar to what they experienced when they pushed the button on the GPS. With a sudden jolt, he was yanked back against the red vinyl seat. He looked down at his lap, wondering what was happening. The force tugging his body backward was so strong he thought he was going to break through the seat and end up in Shorty's booth.

"Do you need to get out?" Ben asked, sliding over.

"I can't—I can't move," Zack stammered, straining to be released before being pulled back again.

Carly saw his jerking movements and the strange look on his face. "What are you doing?" she said in a low voice. "If you don't stop banging against the seat, he's going to notice us."

Zack's eyelids fluttered and he shrugged his shoulders.

"What's the matter with you?" she said as firmly as she could while still maintaining a whisper.

"I'm not sure, but I think The Lincoln has been activated in some way," he finally said.

"What do you mean activated?" Kevin asked with concern.

"It's vibrating and lifting me out of my seat." He tried to explain, but stopped when a sizable man walked into the restaurant. The man was dressed in a black suit that fit well, aside from the top button of his white shirt, which was concealed by his double chin. He sauntered across the diner, mindlessly knocking chairs to the side to allow him to fit through the aisle.

"Well done, Shorty," the man commended as he approached. It was clear he wasn't going to fit in the booth, so he leaned against the back of the seat across from Shorty and remained standing.

"The Senate hearings went off without a hitch. The diversion of all of those letters from concerned taxpayers was a big help. The committee submitted only one hundred letters to support their case."

He stopped as he looked around for the waitress, who was nowhere in sight.

Carly leaned in, waving to the others to come in closer. "This is what I told you about. I found this in my research. Remember Mr. Thomas said the thief's target was a box headed for the Senate?" She spoke so quietly that Zack couldn't hear what she said, but Ben and Kevin both nodded.

The man gave up on the waitress and continued. "The television broadcasters are grateful to you for helping them defend their First Amendment rights. Who cares if they turn a bunch of kids into juvenile delinquents?"

"Just be sure they pay up," Shorty grunted.

The large man slid an envelope across the table. Shorty snatched it up and looked inside. "This better be all of it."

"It is," the man assured him. "I need a job done next week," he said as he moved to leave.

"You know where to find me." Shorty was moving the box to the top of the table when the man grabbed his arm.

"Of course, you'll never speak of our little arrangement," the man told him.

"What arrangement?" Shorty said, jerking his arm back.

"Now, that's what I'm talking about." The man smirked. "I'd hate to have my reputation tarnished."

Zack could see the man lift the top of the box and look inside.

"Ah, there must be over a thousand letters in here. If these had made it to the Senate, the results of that hearing would have been much different." The man laughed, replacing the lid.

Shorty placed a package the size of a hardcover book wrapped in brown paper on top of the box. Zack's body was jerked higher in his seat.

"What's this?" the man asked.

"You wanted what was in the delivery truck—this was it," Shorty said.

The man pushed the box further onto the table and unwrapped the package. "It's a collection of coins," he said as he pulled the paper away from the tablet.

"They must be special if they were put in a plaque," Shorty remarked.

"I think you're right, they must be real special. My nephew would get a kick out of having one of these pennies. Oh, that guy at Ford mentioned he was a coin collector." The man's voice drifted off as he talked to himself. He took one of the coins from the tablet and tossed it to Shorty. "Here you go, Shorty—consider it a tip."

"A penny's the kind of tip I'd expect from you."

"It might be worth something," the man added, putting the tablet inside the box and carrying it out of the restaurant.

Zack held on to the table as tight as he could. It took all his strength to keep the unknown force from pulling him out of the booth and joining the man in the suit. The less intense tugging coming from Shorty's direction was the only thing keeping him in his seat.

"We should go after him," Carly said.

"No, stay here. Look," Ben whispered, pointing at the window where they could see the man putting the box in his car. "There's no way we'd be able to follow him."

Zack felt a tightness in his throat, and his eyes began to water. *What's going on?* He had given everything he had to avoid being pulled into Shorty's booth. With no strength left he folded his arms on the table and put his head down, trying to hide his tears. After a moment, he sniffled and lifted his head, wiping his face on his shirt. He opened his eyes to see Carly, staring at him with her eyebrows furrowed. Too weak to say anything, he let his head drop back onto his arms.

"Would you like some more coffee?" the waitress asked Shorty.

"Yes ma'am," Shorty replied.

She kept his cup full for the next two hours, as he entertained a variety of visitors. Most of them wanted money. Apparently, Shorty was a gambler, and not a very lucky one. He dug inside his envelope and paid nearly everyone that came to see him. Finally, he drained his cup, left a generous tip, and exited the restaurant. Before Zack had a chance to grab hold of the table, The Lincoln yanked him toward the door, pulling him across the seat and knocking him into Ben, sending them both flying out of the booth.

"What's going on with you and The Lincoln?" Ben asked, as they slid back into the seat.

"Nothing now that the other coins are gone, but that was the longest two hours of my life," Zack said. "The Lincoln was attracted to those coins. I could barely hold it back."

"Well, let's hope that's all it was. We can't afford to have any problems with The Lincoln. We still have to get home," Kevin said.

"Did anyone get the name of the guy in the suit?" Zack asked.

"They never said it," Ben replied.

"Maybe Earl will know," Carly suggested.

Zack looked at the clock hanging on the wall. "We'll have to come back tomorrow to ask him. He said he was getting off work at five. That was a half an hour ago."

"I'm going to see if he's still there," Carly said, scooting out of the booth. "I'll be right back."

As she approached the neighboring building, she caught some movement out of the corner of her eye. She turned to look, and a hand grabbed her from behind, forcing her into the empty doorway. She started to scream, but a hand covered her mouth.

"Make a sound and you're dead." Carly recognized the voice.

The stench of cigarettes on Shorty's hand made her gag. Her eyes darted to the street, looking for help, but even though the passersby were only a few feet away, he had her tucked into a doorway where they couldn't be seen. He dug his fingers into her arm, holding her so tight that she couldn't move. His hand fell away from her mouth and she whimpered in pain.

"I told you not to make a sound." His hand that had covered her mouth was now holding a knife. "WHY ARE YOU FOLLOWING ME?" Shorty snarled.

"I'm not following you," she whispered, feeling the tickle of the sharp blade against her throat.

"I saw you in the diner, and here you are coming after me."

Her eyes darted from side to side as she tried to think of what she should say.

"What? You think I wouldn't notice a pretty little thing like you in your fancy clothes? I want to know who sent you. Is it the senator? 'Cause if he wants those photographs, he's gonna have to pay for them."

"I'm not here for anyone but myself," she whined. "I'm looking for my dad." She saw a glimmer of light catch the blade of the knife and reflect onto the wall.

"You think I'm your daddy?" Shorty snorted.

"No. My dad is missing and I'm trying to find him," she said, hoping that if Shorty knew the reason she was there, he would let her go.

"I want to know why you are following me," he demanded, ignoring her explanation.

His arm tightened around her waist, and she could feel the money belt she was wearing dig into her stomach.

"Are you wired?" he asked, poking the straps of the money belt.

"No," she answered.

"Then what's this?" He clenched her shirt and exposed a waistband with zippers.

After their first trip, she'd vowed to always be prepared. Money helps, but only if you can use it. She was carrying three hundred dollars of mixed bills from three different years, in hopes that it would cover them in whatever unexpected situation they may find themselves.

Shorty unzipped one of the compartments and pulled out a wad of money. "I know you're working for someone, and this proves it. Is this the payoff for following me?" He tried to rip the money belt off of her, but the bands around her waist were secure. With his knife, he cut the straps and pushed her to the ground.

"The next time I see you, you're dead," he warned, jumping over her. He took off running with the money belt, leaving her lying half in the doorway and half on the sidewalk. She put her hand on her neck and felt something wet. She was bleeding.

It was only a few seconds before Ben, Kevin, and Zack came running toward her, asking questions. "What happened? What's the matter with your neck? We need to get you to a hospital."

"No," she cried. "Give me your handkerchief so I don't get blood on my shirt." The three of them reached for their handkerchiefs that she'd made them carry as part of their '50s attire.

"Tell me what happened!" Ben demanded.

She sat in the doorway, still frightened and teary, as she told them everything she'd just experienced.

"You could've gotten yourself killed. Don't ever go off by yourself again!" Ben scolded. She could see how furious he was. "If I ever see Shorty again, I'll rip his head off," he declared.

"Oh, you'll see him again," Zack promised. "From what she's saying, Shorty doesn't know anything about our dads, so he's no help there, but he does have one of the coins, and we have to find a way to get it from him."

"That will have to be done on another trip," Kevin said. "We've got to get home. We've been gone way too long."

CHAPTER TWENTY-ONE

LONG NIGHT

Carly

They turned down the first street that they reached to get away from the crowded main street. In search of a private place, they came across an alley where, barring a delivery truck, there was no one around.

"Let's go over there." Zack pointed to a cluster of trash dumpsters.

The stench from the trash was so strong, Carly pinched her nose to keep from gagging.

"Why did we have to come over here? It stinks," she complained.

"This is only going to take a minute," Zack said as he put The Lincoln into the GPS and began toggling through the letters as quickly as he could.

"Hey, you kids," someone yelled. "What are you doing over there?"

They jumped at the sound of the voice and looked behind them to see the driver of the delivery truck walking over to them.

"We've got to go," Kevin yelled to Zack.

Zack immediately held out the handle of the GPS for the others to grab on to before pushing the button. They cringed as a loud ringing sound filled their ears, and through the cloudiness of the magnetic field, they watched the man getting closer. The sensation of spinning made them dizzy, and they closed their eyes. Seconds later, they fell to the ground.

+++++++++

"Where are we?" Kevin asked.

They looked around to see they were all alone in a rather large park with an open entrance at one end and a narrow opening between two chain-linked fences at the other. Their landing must have caused a big gust of wind, because the merry-go-round was spinning like a top.

"I don't recognize this place," Ben said, as they got to their feet.

"Give me the device," Kevin demanded.

Zack handed Kevin the GPS, and he looked closely at the screen.

"You didn't put in all of the letters. We're in Calabash, North Carolina, at 11:30 p.m.," he said before looking closer. "At least you got the year right."

"I didn't put in that location," Zack said.

"Computers don't make mistakes, only people do," Kevin stated as he entered the correct information into the device.

Once again, they heard a loud voice directed at them.

"Hey, you kids, what are you doing over there?"

It was definitely not the same voice they'd heard in Washington DC. They couldn't tell where it was coming from, until they saw the outline of a man at the park entrance. Kevin moved slightly behind Zack so the GPS couldn't be seen.

"Oh great!" Zack said. "Who's this?"

"I can't get the information in fast enough," Kevin said, frantically turning the toggle knob.

"You need to stop, he's coming," Ben told Kevin.

It was the middle of the night and although it was dark, the streetlights provided enough light to see that the man coming toward them was a police officer.

"What are you kids doing?" the officer repeated.

Kevin slipped the device into Zack's backpack.

Carly leaned in. "I have an idea. Let me do the talking," she whispered. "Maybe we can get these '50s clothes to work for us."

"Don't make me ask you again!" the officer called out forcefully.

"I'm sorry, sir," Carly apologized as they approached the officer. "We didn't hear you."

"What are you doing out at this hour?" he asked.

"Our drama club is performing *Grease* and our rehearsal ran late. We're just on our way home," she explained.

He stared at them suspiciously as he walked around, inspecting each one.

"That would explain the clothes," he finally said. "We've been having a problem with vandals in the area. You don't have spray paint in that bag of yours?"

"No, sir," Zack replied.

"Let me take a look," the officer said, holding out his hand.

Zack caught Ben's eye as he slowly slid the backpack off of his shoulder.

"Did you read the sign on the front gate before you came in? This park is closed to the public at 9:00 p.m. and reopens at 7:00 a.m. There's a two hundred and fifty dollar fine for violators," he said. Still holding out his hand, he pointed at Zack's backpack and snapped his fingers. "Hand it over."

"It's late and we wanted to get home, so we were taking a shortcut through the park," Carly explained. "We didn't mean to break any laws, sir."

Zack handed the officer his backpack, and the officer glanced inside. "If you were in such a hurry, why were you on the merry-go-round?" he asked as it slowly came to a stop.

"We weren't," Kevin began, but was interrupted by Zack coughing.

"I just gave it a shove when we went by," Zack explained.

"Hmm. At least one night a week there's a problem in this park," the officer grunted. "I need to set an example, and I'm afraid the four of you are it. I'm going to have to take you down to the station, at which point your parents will be called to pick you up."

"No!" they all shouted at once.

Carly didn't know if the policeman was serious or just trying to scare them, but she wasn't about to take any chances.

"Do you have to go to all that trouble, Officer? We just live around the corner. We didn't do anything wrong." Her voice cracked, sounding as though she was about to cry. "Are you sure you can't just give us a warning?" she begged. "Our parents will kill us if they have to pick us up from the police station."

"Sorry, kid, it's your doing. You shouldn't be roaming around in the middle of the night."

"We're not roaming around," she cried. "We're trying to get home."

Carly started to panic. There were no parents in North Carolina for the police to call. If he took them to the police station, they were going to be in big trouble, and with the officer holding the GPS, there was no way they'd be able to escape.

"Seriously, Officer, we'll be grounded for the rest of our lives if you take us to the police station."

"You leave me with no choice. There's nothing to substantiate your story," the officer said.

"Wait a minute," Carly said. "I know what might convince you. What if we perform one of the numbers from the play right here? That would prove we're telling the truth."

Not knowing what Carly was talking about, Zack and Kevin looked at each other and shrugged their shoulders. But she could tell Ben knew exactly where she was going with this, because he began vehemently shaking his head.

"I don't know," the police officer said, looking around to see if it would cause a disturbance.

"I'm sure you don't want to see us do that," Ben told the officer before turning to face Carly and mouthing, "I'm not doing it."

"Oh, please!" she begged the officer. "It'll prove we're telling the truth."

"No, really!" Ben insisted, glaring at Carly.

The officer made his decision. "That may put this to rest," he said, stepping back and folding his arms on his chest. "Go on then."

Zack's and Kevin's eyes were darting around, unsure of what to do.

Carly looked at Ben with his head and shoulders drooping in defeat. "Ready?" she asked.

The scowl on his face told her he was fuming, and she wondered if he would play along. All she knew for sure was that they had to get out of there, and this was their only chance. Carly cleared her throat and put her head down, shaking her hands at her side. She took a couple of deep breaths, held her head up high, and strutted up to Ben, stopping when she was directly in front of him. She poked him in the chest and began to sing.

You better shape up
'Cause I need a man
And my heart is set on you

You better shape up
You better understand
To my heart I must be true

He succumbed to her crazy idea and halfheartedly tried to keep up with her, nearly tripping when she passed in front of him and flubbing most of his lines. Carly was surprised how well she remembered a dance routine from so many years ago. She gave it all she had, trying to convince the officer to let them go.

While Ben and Carly were singing and skipping around the open space, Zack and Kevin stood with their eyes wide and their mouths gaping, appearing shocked by what they were witnessing.

As they hit the last, "You're the one that I want," the police officer applauded.

"We still need a little work," Carly said, glancing at Ben. "And of course, there's a costume change for that number," she pointed out, catching her breath, winded from the performance.

"That was wonderful!" the police officer raved. "If the other kids are half as good as the two of you, that's going to be some show."

"Thank you, Officer," Carly said.

"Listen, I'm going to let the four of you off this time, but next time I won't be so nice," the officer told them firmly, handing Zack his backpack. "Go ahead now, run along home."

"Thank you so much! We'll go straight home," Carly promised.

They walked out of the main entrance of the park as fast as they could without breaking into a run. Once they turned the corner, they slowed down.

"It's disturbing to watch someone be so deceitful. I guess we're lucky to have someone on our side that can look a police officer straight in the eye and tell a bold-faced lie," Zack said, echoing Carly's earlier words.

"I wouldn't talk if I were you," Carly warned. "I just got us out of a heap of trouble."

"Okay you two, knock it off!" Ben snapped. "Let's go home. And Carly, don't ever ask me to do that again, 'cause I won't do it!"

"Dude, nice dancing." Zack laughed.

Ben pointed in Zack's direction. "Not another word."

They made sure to put some distance between themselves and the police officer before Kevin removed the GPS from Zack's backpack and finished inputting the appropriate time, date, and place.

"We are not getting any sleep tonight. By my calculations, we don't have much time before Mom will be on her way out to the guesthouse. We're cutting it close," Kevin warned as they all gripped the handle, and he pushed the button.

The GPS began to shudder, and they all felt the odd sensation of their teeth vibrating. A piercing ringing sound immediately followed, and they saw the churning iridescent purple line forming around them. They closed their eyes as they began to spin. Within seconds, they were on the ground.

+++++++++

"Now where are we?" Zack asked.

They had landed on a bed of damp, well-manicured grass. A light fog hugged the trees and hovered over the ground around them. The sun had begun to rise and in the not-too-far-off distance, they could see a flagstick stuck into a grassy mound surrounded by water on one side and trees on the other.

"I think we're on the eighteenth fairway at the club," Ben said, looking around.

"It's already six o'clock, and if that's true, we're never going to make it. We'd better run for it," Kevin said.

They took off toward the clubhouse, racing across the stone

bridge and up the hill. As they got closer they could see Jim standing near some golf carts.

"Head for the carts," Zack called out.

They ran as fast as they could. Ben was the first one to get there. He leaned against one of the carts, trying to catch his breath.

"Jim, we're in trouble," he panted. "We need to get home quick."

The others caught up, gasping for air.

"You've figured out what your fathers have been up to, haven't you?" Jim asked.

"Yes," Ben answered quickly. "But we are not nearly as good at it. Can we borrow a cart?"

"The cart barn closes at seven. Make sure you have it back by then," he said, and when you have time, I'd love to hear what's going on."

"Not sure that we can tell you," Ben said as he and Zack hopped into the nearest cart.

"If you get caught, I'll deny knowing anything about it," Jim warned, as he unplugged the GPS on the cart.

Kevin and Carly jumped onto the back and grabbed hold of the roof.

"We'll bring the cart back after school," Zack assured him.

"Like I said, I don't know anything about it." Jim turned his back to them and headed for the pro-shop.

"Hang on," Zack yelled to the others from the driver's seat as they made their way through the parking lot. The gate was open, and the security guard was not yet on duty. They sped through the exit and turned right at the street.

"Is this as fast as this thing can go?" Carly yelled from the back.

"We're going uphill. When we start going down, you'd better hold on, 'cause if you fall off, I'm not stopping," Zack replied.

As he said that, they were over the hill and accelerating on the downhill side. He turned the corner so fast the cart nearly tipped over.

"Whoa!" Kevin screamed, holding on for dear life.

They drove down their street, hoping that no one in the few passing cars recognized them. When they reached the Marshall house, they pulled in beside the garage.

"Our bikes," Carly yelled, thinking Zack was going to crash into them.

"They're still on Topanga," Ben told her. "We have a lot to do after school."

Zack pulled the cart up far enough to not be visible from the street. They snuck in the back gate and slipped into the guesthouse.

"Leave the door cracked so we can hear what's going on," Zack instructed. "There's no time to change clothes. We'll have to make do, so we'd better get presentable."

They straightened their clothes, and Carly checked her scarf that she had moved from her ponytail to her neck to hide the cut left by Shorty's knife. They heard the door to the main house open.

Zack closed his eyes and shook his head. "I hope we're not busted!"

Sharon entered the guesthouse, eyeing their clothes. "It must be '50s day. You guys look great," she said.

"Thank you," Carly replied, adjusting her ponytail in the mirror.

"Kevin, are they having '50s day at the middle school as well?" Sharon asked.

"Mom, you know he has to do everything I do," Zack said.

"Breakfast is almost ready, so come up to the house. Aunt Tina gave me her frittata recipe," Sharon told them.

They all breathed a sigh of relief and followed her to the house.

++++++++++

Zack

After dropping Kevin off at the middle school, Sharon pulled up in front of the high school.

"It's so disappointing to see such a lack of school spirit," she said, watching the students entering the school.

"What, Mom?" Zack asked from the backseat.

"It doesn't look like many students are participating in '50s day," she replied.

Zack and Ben gave each other a look.

"I'm sure there's loads more kids dressed up that are already inside," Carly remarked, as she opened her door.

They got out of the SUV as fast as they could before Sharon could make any more observations. Carly went straight to her locker, while Ben and Zack headed for class, still amazed at how close they had cut it that morning.

Math class proved to be the same old boring stuff. So boring in fact that halfway through, Zack stood his book up and put his head down on his desk. Within seconds, he was sound asleep. *SPLAT!* He awoke with a start. His book was lying on the floor and Mr. Baumgart seemed to tower over him.

"Are we putting you to sleep, Mr. Marshall?" he snarled.

"I'm sorry . . . my dad . . ." Zack groggily searched for an explanation.

Mr. Baumgart interrupted. "I wondered how long it would take for you to use that as an excuse. Follow me to the front of the class."

It may have been morning, but Zack was still living the longest night of his life. He slowly got up and followed his teacher to the front of the class.

Mr. Baumgart stood at the chalkboard, writing out an equation, then leaned back with a smug look on his face, waiting to criticize

Zack's inability to solve the problem. Zack walked up to the blackboard, looked at the equation, grabbed a piece of chalk, and wrote out the answer. The classroom grew completely silent. Zack stood there, trying not to smile. The teacher's scheme to humiliate him in front of the class usually worked, but not this time. Zack wasn't sure exactly what the blue light had shared with him that made math so easy, but whatever it was, he sure appreciated it. He closed his hand around The Lincoln in his pocket. *Thank you!*

Mr. Baumgart stepped between Zack and the chalkboard, analyzing the numbers Zack had written. His stunned reaction to Zack's correct answer lasted only a second before he quickly put his chalk to the board, challenging Zack with an even more difficult problem. Zack had no calculator or worksheet, only the chalk in his hand as he stood there in his retro outfit, looking half-asleep. Without hesitation, he wrote the answer.

Mr. Baumgart continued to compile equation after equation on the chalkboard, only for Zack to instantly jot down the answers. When Mr. Baumgart had filled the entire chalkboard, he stopped. "Get out of my classroom now!" he bellowed.

The room erupted with applause. Zack went to his desk and grabbed his backpack, and before reaching the door, he turned and bowed to a still cheering room of classmates. Moments later, the bell rang and everyone spilled out into the hallway.

"I don't think you have to worry about Baumgart anymore," Ben told Zack.

"You're wrong," Zack replied, knowing that Baumgart was going to make him pay for what just happened. "I'm sure my problems with him just got way worse."

The show Zack put on in Baumgart's class spread like wildfire. At lunch, the student body buzzed with news of Zack putting "Bum" in his place.

Ben and Zack finally made their way through the cafeteria to their usual table, where Carly was waiting.

"How's it goin'?" Ben asked.

Carly shrugged her shoulders. "Just a bit tired," she said before turning to Zack. "I knew one day that loser Baumgart would pick on the wrong kid. I just never guessed that kid would be you."

++++++++++

After school, they retrieved their bikes and returned the golf cart to the club. When they got back to the Marshall home, Sharon pulled Zack aside while the others headed for the guesthouse.

"What have you done now?" she demanded.

So much had happened in the last twelve hours, he wasn't exactly sure what she was talking about.

"Your teacher, Mr. Baumgart, called again. Really Zack, don't you think things are bad enough right now? Do you have to make it even more difficult?"

"I didn't do anything wrong," he defended.

She put her hand on her hip and gave him a disbelieving look.

"All I did was answer some math problems on the chalkboard," he stated, irritated by the expression on his mother's face.

"Well, you must have done more than that," she said. "Because you're not to return to Mr. Baumgart's class until we meet with him and the principal on Monday."

"Good!" he shouted. "I hope I never have to go back to his class again!" He stomped out, slamming the door on his way to the guesthouse.

CHAPTER TWENTY-TWO

WHO'S TO BLAME?

Zack

"Don't forget that you're spending first period in the principal's office today and tomorrow," Sharon told Zack as she pulled her SUV in front of the school.

"I know, Mom," Zack said, rolling his eyes as he got out. "How could I forget?"

Carly and Ben closed their doors, and the three of them rushed into the building. Carly headed for her locker, while Ben opened the door to Baumgart's class, and Zack continued down the hall. The bell rang as he approached the office counter, where he recognized Emily, the student aide working behind the desk.

"Hi, I was told to come here instead of going to math class."

"Good morning," Emily replied with a smile. She didn't need to ask his name. She knew exactly who he was. "Did you have a little problem in Baumgart's class?"

"You could say that," he said, returning her smile.

Zack remembered Emily from middle school but hadn't seen much of her lately, as she tended to be in the more advanced classes.

She pushed a piece of paper toward him. "Sign here," she said, looking at the computer. "Sorry, but you'll have to come here tomorrow as well." The smile returned to her face.

"No reason to be sorry. I'm sure hanging out here will be better than what I've been doing first period," Zack replied, turning to have a seat.

Zack sat down on the couch and stretched out his arms as he leaned back. "Ah." *I should have gotten kicked out of class sooner.* He unzipped his backpack and pulled out his Spanish homework. The hour flew by, and the rest of the morning was a breeze until he saw his baseball teammate Justin in the lunchroom.

"Man, you have to come back to the team," Justin told him, shaking his head. "We've lost every game since you've been out. We need you."

Zack couldn't believe what he was hearing. *How could he not know that I'd rather be playing baseball than going through all this other crap!* Justin seemed to be talking a mile a minute. Zack's frustration was coming to a head, and still Justin kept talking.

"Dylan's been pulled off of the team until he brings his grades up. We'll be graduating before that happens." Justin rolled his eyes. "I mean it! Why don't you skip practice and just play the games? I'm sure the coach will make an exception."

"It's not like I don't want to play baseball. I just can't right now!" he practically yelled at Justin before storming away.

Zack considered his own words. *How long is "right now" going to last?* he wondered. *We know where one coin is, but that's not telling us where our dads are. They risked their lives for years searching for these coins. Is that what we've signed up for?* He stopped and closed his eyes. His head dropped, thinking of what Mr. Thomas said. "*When you find the coins, you will find your fathers.*" A pain flared in his stomach.

++++++++++

At the end of the school day, Zack, Ben, Carly, and Kevin met in the guesthouse to devise a plan.

"First, we get the coin from Shorty," Zack said.

"How are we supposed to do that?" Kevin asked.

"We're going to have to find out where Shorty lives and search the place," Zack replied.

"That's crazy," Carly said.

"What do *you* suggest we do?" Zack questioned, irritated by her response.

"Well, nothing that would involve breaking and entering!"

"Okay, go ahead and tell us what you suggest," Zack pressed as he folded his arms and waited.

Carly let out a deep breath as she thought. "Well, we could tell Shorty that we want to buy the coin and let him name his price," she finally replied. "If I could buy a soda for ten cents, I'm sure there's enough money in Dad's safe to cover any amount that Shorty might ask for." She looked at Ben and he nodded.

"Shorty already thinks you're spying on him. He's not going to sell you anything," Zack told her.

"We can't all go up to him together. Someone has to do it alone," Kevin suggested.

"I'll do it. I'll get the coin from him one way or another," Ben said, forming a fist.

"Okay, that's really stupid!" Carly told him. "You said something like that the other day, too. You never used to talk like that. You're starting to sound like him," she said, pointing at Zack.

Zack opened his mouth to defend himself, but Ben spoke before he could. "You're the one that sounds stupid!" Ben yelled.

Carly's eyebrows shot up and she tossed her hair back. Zack

smirked. All he needed was some popcorn.

"You don't get it," Ben told her. "We were crushed when Mom died, and now look, the same thing is going to happen to Dad, but this time we'll be left with no one." Blotches of red formed on his face as he continued. "Oh sure, we're out there trying to find him, but what if we don't? We're going to lose him too, and this time it'll be way worse, because it'll be our fault that we didn't save him."

"It will not be our fault," she spouted back.

"Okay, if you want to be technical about it, I guess we can blame Shorty, can't we? He's the one robbing people without caring whose lives he destroys. If he wouldn't have stolen the tablet with the coins to begin with, we wouldn't be having this discussion right now."

Carly didn't say a word.

"So yes, I'll gladly offer to buy the coin, and if he doesn't go along with it, I'm willing to do whatever it takes to get it from him."

"That's ridiculous!" She deepened her voice. "You're acting like this is the last straw and you're out to get him."

"I don't know where you got that. All I'm saying is that guy is a scumbag and he deserves to be brought down," Ben told her.

"Yeah, but not by you," Carly said.

Ben threw his hands in the air and stormed out of the guesthouse, slamming the door behind him. Carly didn't follow.

CHAPTER TWENTY-THREE

'ROUND MIDNIGHT

Zack

Friday finally arrived, and with the school day behind them, Ben and Zack sat in the guesthouse with the maps laid out on the table.

"Make sure you keep Kevin and Carly out of the line of fire tonight," Ben said.

"I will, and you'd better watch your back. That guy is dangerous," Zack replied.

"Together we'd for sure be able to take him, if we had to," Ben pointed out.

"Yeah, let's hope we don't have to," Zack said. "I don't know what my dad was thinking putting us in this position, or yours either. They must've known what they were getting us into by sending us The Lincoln."

"I can't even guess what was going through their heads. I feel like I don't even know my dad after finding out all this crap about the coins. Our whole lives we've grown up surrounded by secrets and lies. Even after my mom died, he still didn't fess up," Ben said. "This whole thing is unreal."

"They've both got a lot of explaining to do when we get them home," Zack said.

"They sure do," Ben said, looking at the clock.

Zack's eyes followed his. "It's time. Let's go load your gear."

++++++++++

Carly

Sharon pulled up to the school.

"It will take about an hour to tear down after the dance, so you can pick us up around midnight," Ben informed Sharon.

"Call me when you're ready," Sharon told them.

They unloaded Ben's gear and carried it into the gymnasium. Carly looked around and was shocked at the transformation. In keeping with the spring theme, flowers were placed everywhere. Lights that had been strung overhead were twinkling, and loud music pulsed through the PA system. A table was set up with assorted beverages and snacks next to a sign that read "$5."

The door opened, and she turned to see band member Adam, approaching.

"I have to hand it to the student council, they've made this place look great," Carly stated.

"Yeah, I barely recognize the dump," Adam agreed.

Carly laughed. "You're here early," she said, examining Adam's sandy blond hair, which was messier than usual and held that way by some super-hold substance.

"The drummer's curse… first one in, last one out," he told her.

"Need help unloading?" Ben asked.

"Sure," Adam replied, leading Ben, Zack, and Kevin out to the parking lot where they ended up helping Taylor and Brandon unload their equipment as well.

While the band was setting up, Zack discretely taped the latch of the exit door to ensure they could get back in if they returned late.

Slowly, the room began to fill with friends and fellow students. It was a great turnout, and when everything was set, the members of the band took their place on stage.

"Welcome to the Spring Fling," Ben announced into the microphone.

The audience applauded and gathered around the front of the stage. Taylor motioned to the other band members, acknowledging that the producer they'd invited was standing in the back of the room. Ben planned on making a good impression and chose a song written by Adam that had roused the audience during their last gig. When the band was set, Adam counted off and Ben sang.

> My friends all warned me
> Don't get too close to you
> But they will see
> What I always knew
>
> I want to be more
> Than just your friend
> I know you must think
> I'm on the mend
> But you're not a rebound
> I think its love
> That we've found

When I'm with you, girl
I want to make a new start
Take it slow, girl
Don't break my heart

When I see you, baby
The one that I want now is you
And I trust you, baby
I know that you feel it too

As the last words left Ben's lips, he froze. Carly saw him just standing there, and wondered what the matter was. His eyes were locked on someone in the audience, but she couldn't see who it was. Adam tapped his sticks together to get Ben's attention. When the band began the next song, Ben put his guitar on a stand and left the stage.

Carly was the first person he ran into.

"Why didn't you tell me she was coming?" Ben yelled over the blaring music.

"Who? What are you talking about?"

"Frankie," he shouted angrily.

"Francesca's here? Where?" Carly asked, standing on her tiptoes to try to see around him.

"Did you tell her that I would be here tonight?"

"No, why would I do that?"

He looked at the sea of heads in front of the stage and turned back to Carly. His face was covered with red blotches. His eyes were narrowed into slits, and his lips were moving. She leaned in, straining to hear what he was saying.

"In case you're wondering, *this* is the last straw," he growled.

Zack and Kevin rushed over to them. "What are you guys doing? Let's go!"

They hurried out of the room into the hallway.

"I can't believe I picked that song," Ben said out loud to himself as he headed toward the exit. "Why did she have to be here?"

He stopped, balled his hand into a fist, and punched a locker as hard as he could.

The others stopped in their tracks, exchanging looks of surprise. Ben stormed out of the building, pushing the door open so hard it nearly cracked the window when it hit the other side. Carly, Zack, and Kevin were still standing in the same spot when the door reopened.

"Are you coming?" Ben yelled.

They all looked at each other and followed him out of the building.

"What's up?" Zack asked. "Are you okay?"

"Let's just go," Ben replied, pacing back and forth and shaking his head.

Carly handed out shirts and they put them on over the T-shirts they were wearing. They changed their shoes and hid the ones they had been wearing in a bag under some oleander bushes. Kevin programmed the GPS and Zack put The Lincoln in place. Wasting no time, he held it out for the others to grab hold.

Zack pushed the button, and their shoulders tensed as they fought the pain of the earsplitting screech that filled their ears. With their eyes shut tight, no one even saw the purple line forming around them as they began to spin. Seconds later, they hit the ground hard. It was 3:00 p.m. on June 24, 1954, and they landed in the same location as every other time they'd traveled to Washington, DC. Quickly leaving the seclusion of the pine trees, they were on their way to the diner, hoping Shorty would be there.

CHAPTER TWENTY-FOUR

UP A RIVER

Carly

The street was bustling with businesspeople, shoppers, and tourists. They passed a government building with large white pillars and a grassy area with a pole flying an American flag. They crossed the street and were approaching the barbershop when Earl came out to meet them.

"I hoped you would come," he said. "Everybody's going nuts around here. Shorty's in big trouble."

"What kind of trouble?" Carly asked.

"I'll tell you all about it. First, let me go ask Mr. Brock if I can take a break. I'll meet you in the diner."

They walked to the corner and entered the diner, sitting down at a table just inside the front door. Carly noticed Ben had seated himself at the far end of the table. He was staring out of the window with his arm on the table, tapping his finger as his jaw muscles pulsed.

"Earl better be quick. We've got to get out of here before Shorty gets here," Zack said as the waitress approached the table.

Everyone except Ben ordered a soda. Only a few minutes passed before Earl joined them and looked over at Ben.

"Is he okay?" Earl asked.

"Yeah," Zack replied. "What's going on with Shorty?"

Earl quickly filled them in. "This morning, Shorty was Mr. Brock's first haircut and shave. He must have won playing poker last night, because he was as happy as a lark. He gave Mr. Brock a five-dollar bill for a seventy-five-cent service, and told him to keep the change." His voice lowered and his eyes got big. "Mr. Brock's next customer, who's the head of the FBI, saw this, and when he was finished said he wished he could be as generous as the last patron, but needed nine dollars back from his ten. Mr. Brock gave the man four singles and the five-dollar bill Shorty had given him. The man took a good look at the money and saw that the five-dollar bill was counterfeit." Earl slapped his hand on the table. "Can you believe that? Just a little while ago another one of Mr. Brock's customers said that the authorities have been following Shorty all day, watching him spread bad money all over town."

Carly remembered trying to pay for a soda on their first trip and the clerk referring to her five-dollar bill as play money.

"I heard one of the senators say that the police have been after Shorty for years, but haven't been able to pin anything on him," Earl continued. "Now with the federal authorities involved, they're looking to send Shorty up a river without a paddle. Though they do have to catch him first."

Just as Earl finished his story, Ben jumped up so fast his chair fell backward. He pushed through the door of the diner and took off running.

"Where's he going?" Carly asked.

As they followed Ben out the door, they heard a car horn blast.

Ben had made his way across the street and was maneuvering between two parked cars on the other side.

"What's he doing?" Carly questioned. She saw Ben run in front of the government building, heading toward a man walking alone on the grass. "Oh my God, is that Shorty?" she yelled.

"Yeah, looks like Ben's going after him," Zack said, rushing to the curb and running across the street with the others on his heels.

Carly kept her eyes on Ben as she ran, and watched him plow right into Shorty. Shorty was on the ground, pulling his knife from his pocket, but before he could get to his feet, Ben pushed him face-first into a pillar and his knife flew from his hand.

"Don't ever touch my sister again. Give me the coin," Ben panted, hovering over Shorty. Shorty covered his face to stop the blood flowing from his nose.

Zack ran up to Ben. "Stop." He grabbed Ben's arm and pulled him away.

Carly ran in front of Zack. She didn't notice that Shorty had stood up and was lunging toward her. Ben and Zack turned, but it was too late. Shorty had Carly's arm and was pulling her closer to him. She screamed as he twisted her arm behind her back.

Kevin and Earl had reached them. "CARLY!" Kevin yelled.

"Now hold on there, Shorty!" Earl shouted.

Shorty slowly backed away, dragging Carly with him. His eyes darted toward his knife as he inched closer to it. Carly screamed in pain as Shorty tightened his grip. "I promised the next time I saw you, you'd be dead," he whispered in her ear. "And I don't break promises." He looked up to see Ben moving toward him. "I'll snap her arm right off," he warned. He took another step backward, jerking Carly from side to side and making it impossible for Ben or Zack to get to him.

"Let her go!" Ben yelled.

Suddenly, the sound of squealing tires and police sirens filled the air. Three police cars came to a stop in front of them and opened their doors.

"FBI, drop your weapons," the agent yelled as they drew their guns. "Hands in the air."

They all did what they were told. Shorty mumbled something as he pushed Carly away from him, and she fell to the ground. She scurried toward Ben.

Two FBI agents and a police officer approached them, while the other officers remained behind the opened car doors with their guns aimed at Shorty.

"Cuff him," the agent told the officer.

"Put your hands on the hood of the car," the officer said, shoving Shorty in the direction of the police car. The officer pulled Shorty's arms behind his back, forcing handcuffs onto his wrists.

"You can put your hands down, but keep them where I can see them," the agent told the others. "Lower your weapons." He waved to the officers.

"Earl," one of the FBI agents said, recognizing him from the barbershop, "what are you doing mixed up in this?"

Earl nodded toward Ben.

"I was just trying to stop him from killing Shorty and ending up in jail."

"Lucky for all of you we've been tailing Shorty, or this situation may have ended badly. Earl, you'd better get back to the shop while we sort this out."

"Yes, sir." Earl went back across the street. Mr. Brock was standing in front of the barbershop where a crowd of spectators were gathering.

"Now, tell me, young man," one of the agents said to Ben. "Why were you going after Shorty?"

"He robbed my sister." Ben pointed at Carly. "He held a knife to her throat and threatened her life."

"That's a lie. He's the one who came after me. I've never seen that girl before in my life," Shorty yelled.

Carly untied the scarf, exposing the wound on her neck.

"This cut came from his knife," she said.

"This is looking real bad for you, Shorty. Assault with a deadly weapon." The police officer was obviously enjoying the moment.

"Your brother said you were robbed. What did he take?" the agent asked.

Carly glanced down at the ground and thought for a moment. The dates on the bills Shorty took from her money belt made everyone believe the money was counterfeit. She wasn't about to claim them, but on the other hand, she did want to know if he was still carrying the coin. Looking at her shoes, she had an idea.

"Well, sir, this is going to sound petty, but I didn't have any money so he took my lucky penny from my shoe."

"From your shoe?" the officer said.

"Yes, I keep my lucky penny in the top of my loafer and he took it!" she exclaimed.

"Shorty, you should be ashamed of yourself," the officer said.

"She's a liar. I never took a penny off her shoe," Shorty said.

"It's a 1943 copper penny and I want it back!" Carly shouted at Shorty.

"Let's see if we can't resolve this matter right now. Empty his pockets," the agent told the officer. The officer removed a roll of bills from Shorty's pocket and placed them on the hood of the police car. As he did, a coin hit the ground and rolled across the sidewalk, stopping in front of Zack.

Carly noticed a strange look on Zack's face, and her heart raced as the officer picked up the coin.

"Just as you described, young lady." He handed the coin to the agent.

The agent pointed to the money on the hood of the car. "What do we have here?"

"That's my money," Shorty claimed. "I didn't steal it from her."

"No one has accused you of stealing that money," the agent replied. "Check the dates on those bills," he told the officer.

The officer separated some of the bills on the hood of the car and read the dates out loud. "Series 1962, 1980, and 2000."

"That money is counterfeit. You are under arrest for counterfeiting and racketeering."

Shorty sneered at Carly. "It was a setup. I got that money from her yesterday."

"I thought you never saw her before." The officer laughed as he grabbed Shorty's arm and forced him into the backseat of the police car.

"Tell it to the judge," one of the agents said. His gaze went to Ben and Carly. "We've got who we're after." He nodded toward Shorty in the police car. "But before we let you go, I'll need to get your information."

Once again, Carly's heart raced and she was uncertain what to do. She caught Kevin's eye and he gestured for her to go ahead.

Carly gave the agent her first name as well as Ben's, Zack's, and Kevin's, but gave Watson as their last name. She supplied the agent with the correct city, but fabricated their address.

"Well, I guess that wraps things up," the agent said, putting his notebook in his jacket pocket. "You can go now, and stay out of trouble."

"Ahem." Carly cleared her throat. "May I have my coin back?"

"Yes," the agent said, turning the coin over in his hand. "You should keep it in a more secure place than your shoe if it means that much to you. I also recommend you get a new lucky charm. This one doesn't appear to have brought you much luck."

"Thank you," she said as he placed the coin in her hand.

The four of them walked across the street to where Earl was standing. Mr. Brock returned to work and the crowd dispersed.

"When will you be heading back to California?" Earl asked.

"Our parents are waiting for us now," Carly said.

"Before we go, I want to ask if you saw a man carrying a box out of the diner yesterday?" Zack inquired.

"I was keeping my eye on the place while you were there. I saw Shorty walk in with a box, and Mr. Frederick carry it out."

"Mr. Frederick?" Ben asked.

"He's a lobbyist for some big companies. Right now, he's working for the television companies. Those hearings about comic books and television turning kids into juvenile delinquents were all the talk until this Shorty mess. I don't know how Mr. Frederick did it, but he got those television people off without so much as a slap on the wrist."

"Thanks! You sure know everything that's going on around here, don't you?" Zack said.

"That's what happens in a barbershop—people talk and I listen." Earl smiled.

"Earl, thank you so much for your help." Carly handed him a cream-colored envelope.

"What's this?"

"Just a little something for helping us out," she told him.

"It was nothing." He pulled the front of his shirt collar together with a laugh. "I felt like I was one of those FBI agents."

"Me too," Zack said. "We've got to get going. I hope we meet again." Zack reached out and shook his hand.

The others said goodbye to Earl, and the four of them walked down the street, turning at the corner and heading for the alley.

++++++++++

Zack

Zack was uncontrollably drawn to Carly. He could feel the strength of The Lincoln and realized Kevin hadn't removed the coin from the GPS. He was trying to hold himself apart from her, but lost the battle and snapped against Carly's side like a rubber band, knocking her to the ground.

"What are you doing? Get off me!" she demanded.

Zack got up and offered her his hand and helped her up. "When that coin rolled over to me, I could feel it pulling the backpack, and ever since the agent handed you that coin, it's been pulling me toward you. I've been fighting to hold The Lincoln back, just like in the restaurant. The connection between the pennies is strong. I can feel it—watch." He took off his backpack and placed it on the ground. Immediately, the backpack flew up and hit Carly so hard it knocked her down again.

"Zack, you idiot! I can't believe you just did that!" she yelled.

"Oh, you're not hurt. Get up, you big baby," he laughed. "I didn't know that it would hit you that hard."

"But you knew it would come at me, didn't you? That was real nice," she said, getting to her feet and dusting herself off.

"You're right. After the way you handled Shorty, I shouldn't have done that. I can't believe you got the coin," Zack said as they entered the alley.

"I can't believe it either," Carly said, turning to Ben. "I'm surprised I could even think after the stunt you pulled. What if the police hadn't shown up when they did? You could have gotten killed, or worse, you could have gotten *me* killed." She rubbed her arm.

Ben looked at the ground as they walked. "When Earl told us

about the counterfeit money, I figured if Shorty got arrested, we would never get the coin," he said, attempting to excuse his behavior.

"Still, what you did wasn't cool at all. What's the point of having a plan if you go off and do whatever you want? If we're going to look for the other two coins, we all need to be on the same page and stay on that page!" Carly insisted.

Zack and Kevin felt the same way about Ben's actions, but didn't say anything.

"How did you think of that shoe thing?" Ben asked, changing the subject.

"Something Earl said about the style of my shoes was my first thought. Then I remembered Dad telling Bill he hoped the steel penny that he gave him for his birthday would bring him luck. Shorty was wearing the same clothes as when he got the coin, and I thought there was a chance he may still have it on him. So, I took a shot."

"That was awesome," Kevin said.

"Thank you," she said with a sly smile. "Are we going to have a problem getting this coin home? I mean, can you take something from the past to the future?" she asked, handing the penny to Zack. He felt a mild shock when she dropped it into his hand and quickly put the coin into his back pocket.

"Why wouldn't we be able to?" Ben asked, looking around to make sure they couldn't be seen behind the dumpster.

"Phew, it reeks!" Carly gagged, and her hand went to her nose, attempting to block the stench. "Why do we have to go by the trash bins?"

"Because we're less likely to be seen," Ben replied. "You didn't answer me. Why would you think we'd have a problem taking the coin home?"

"I don't know," she replied, still pinching her nose. "I hadn't thought about it before now. I was just wondering if it breaks some time travel law to take something from one time to another."

"I didn't see anything about that in my research," Zack responded.

"We have to try. We don't have a choice. What's the worst that could happen?" Kevin said as he entered the information into the GPS for the return trip. "Plus, our dads must have done it when they found a coin."

CHAPTER TWENTY-FIVE

GET BACK

Zack

Kevin held out the GPS for everyone to take hold of, before pushing the button. Their bodies tensed, but the usual ear-splitting sound that they were anticipating was replaced by a deafening silence. They watched the churning iridescent purple line and the dome form around them. Suddenly, they began floating.

Suspended in darkness, they defied gravity, seeing what looked like millions of stars. A magnificent display of red, yellow, violet, and green hung in the sky like colorful cloud formations. A few rays of white light shined brightly through the spectacle.

Suddenly they were jolted backward, then pulled forward. It felt as though they were on a turbulent plane ride without the plane. A moment later, they slowed and were floating once again. The night sky was gone, and they shielded their eyes from the brightness of the sun.

Through the haze of the magnetic field that surrounded them, they looked down at a black Range Rover parked in a clearing on a mountain road. While hovering invisibly above the scene, they saw a black car with darkened windows enter the parking lot, followed by a white van that stopped directly behind the Range Rover.

"That's them!" Carly yelled.

Zack watched her as she tried to break away. It was the first time the bracelets that Carly made were tested, and they worked just like he predicted. Each of their hands seemed to be glued to the handle of the GPS.

The Range Rover doors opened, and they watched their dads get out and walk over to the two men from the van. They were too far away to hear what was being said, but it was obvious that the four men were having a disagreement. As Bill and Sam attempted to go back to the Range Rover, the shorter of the two men ran after Sam and jumped him from behind, knocking him to the ground. Ben, Carly, Zack, and Kevin began screaming and struggling, each waving their free arm, trying to break through the barrier and help their dads. But it was useless. They watched the taller of the two men pull out a gun and herd their fathers toward the van, while his companion opened the back door. Just before they were both forced into the back of the van, Zack saw a glint of sun reflect off of something his dad dropped to the ground.

Immediately, they were jolted forward and began to spin, losing sight of the lookout. When they stopped, they were still suspended in the air, but the scene at Topanga was gone. Through the mist, they could see the tops of trees below them, alongside a strip of short grass where a small plane had landed. Bill and Sam emerged from the plane with their hands tied and gray tape covering their mouths.

"Dad!" Zack yelled as he watched two men leading their fathers into the woods.

They hovered above the trees, searching for movement below.

Even though many of the trees had no leaves, the tentacles of the dense vines blanketing much of the forest were blowing in the wind, giving false sightings. Finally, the men emerged from the woods next to a large barn. Zack tried to see if there was anything around that might tell him where they were, but only the barn was in focus.

He studied the weathered slats of wood covering the structure. They varied in color from gray to brown, allowing the barn to blend in with the mostly bare branches of the surrounding trees. Filthy nine-pane windows stood on each side of the sizable wood door. At the point of the rooftop, a weathervane with a horse trotting on an arrow squeaked as it moved slightly in the wind.

The kidnapper holding Bill pulled the tape off of his mouth.

"Make as much noise as you want. No one can hear you. When the boss gets here, you'd better tell us everything you know about the coin."

"Never," Bill vowed.

"We can do this the easy way or the hard way. It's up to you," the man told him.

One of the men slid open the large door, while the other forced Bill and Sam into the barn, pushing them to the ground. Zack and Kevin yelled, trying to get their dad's attention, but still could not be heard.

Without warning, whatever was holding the four of them was gone. They screamed as they fell to the earth, coming to an abrupt stop just inches above the ground. It took seconds before they realized the scene had changed. It was night. A light shined through the open barn door. They peered through the opening and saw their dads sitting at a table.

"I want to know what you've done with the coin!" a gruff voice demanded.

"I swear, I don't know where it is," Bill replied.

"You swear? Like that's supposed to mean something to me? I want to know where the coin is right now!"

"I've already told you, it must have fallen out of the watch when your thugs were pushing us around. You have the watch. You can see for yourself it's damaged. There's nothing more I can tell you."

"You haven't been without that coin since the day your father gave it to you," the voice said. "You know where it is, I'm sure of it. I'm not playing games with the two of you anymore. I've treated you well in hopes of getting information from you, but I see I've wasted my time."

There were sounds of movement. Two men came into view. Zack recognized them as the men who brought their dads to the barn.

"Go back to Los Angeles. Find their kids. If they don't have the coin, go after his wife," the gruff voice instructed. "Maybe I'll get some cooperation if we spread the pain around a little."

+++++++++

Carly

A piercingly loud ringing sound jarred their ears and they began to spin. Seconds later, they were dumped onto the hard ground. They were back in Topanga Canyon.

"Oh my God! Did you see them? We have to go back!" Carly yelled. "We have to get back to them right now!"

"We can't go back," Kevin replied. "We're lucky to have made it through the first time."

"What?" Carly said, jerking around to look at him. "You're kidding. Right?"

"No, I'm not! I have no idea how to get back to them," Kevin said, reading the screen of the GPS. "Besides, it's eleven o'clock. We've got to get back to the school."

"We have plenty of time," Ben said.

"You did it once, you can do it again," Zack told Kevin.

"The GPS is programmed for us to get home. I input everything the same as usual."

"It has to be the other coin," Carly said. "It's the only thing that's different."

"Of course it is, but you don't get it," Kevin stressed. "Wormholes are unstable. The additional energy put out by the other coin could've had an effect on our speed, energy density, or even the radial tension of the wormhole itself. There is no way of knowing."

"We need to at least try. Maybe we'll see something that'll help us figure out how to find them," Ben said, ignoring Kevin's warning.

"You're not listening to me! It's too dangerous."

"C'mon Kevin, set that thing for DC, and we'll do it again," Zack demanded.

"I don't think it's smart," Kevin said in frustration.

"Just do it!" Zack shouted.

"Okay, okay."

Kevin scrolled through the letters, entering the address of the Library of Congress. With all of them putting one hand on the handle of the GPS, he pressed the button. There was complete silence and they began to spin. For a moment, Carly thought they were going to be able to see their dads, but after only a second, they dropped down in the middle of three pine trees.

"Now put in our home address," Ben instructed, getting to his feet. "That's the address that was in the GPS when we saw them."

"Yeah, and hurry up," Zack added.

Kevin quickly toggled through the letters and numbers, holding the GPS out for everyone to grab hold. He pushed the button, but they heard nothing. No one dared close their eyes at the risk of missing something. They all saw the purple line forming a circle around them and the electromagnetic shield that sprung from it. Seconds later, they were lying on dead pine needles at the lookout in Topanga Canyon. Disappointed, they remained on the ground. Carly put her hands up to her face to hide the tears streaming down her cheeks.

"It's that stupid bubble around us. It wouldn't let us get to them," Ben said.

"They didn't even know we were there," Carly sniffled.

"We need to find them for real next time," Ben said. "At least we know they're okay for now."

Kevin looked at the time as he removed The Lincoln from the GPS. "We need to get back to the school. Here," he said, handing The Lincoln to Zack. "You'd better carry both coins so The Lincoln doesn't pull you all over the place."

They got to their feet, brushed off the dirt, and started walking.

"Man, nothing looked familiar; not the field where the plane landed, or the barn," Zack said.

"I know, wherever they are, I've never been there before," Ben added as they walked.

"Me either," both Carly and Kevin agreed.

They quickly made their way to the school and retrieved their shoes, sticking their '50s shirts in Zack's backpack. The band was packing up when they entered the gymnasium.

"There you are! Finally, he returns," Adam said, pointing at Ben. "Man, you missed a great gig."

"I'll be there for the next one," Ben promised.

"That's only a week away," Taylor said. "They asked us to play at the prom. I don't know what happened to the DJ they had booked, but the gig is ours now."

"I hope everything's worked out by then," Ben mumbled. "How did it go with the producer?"

"Kenny liked the band and wants to record a couple of the songs we played tonight. He especially liked the first one that you did with us. He's going to check his schedule and wants to get started in the next couple of weeks." Adam looked Ben in the eye and lowered his voice. "I know you have some crazy stuff going on right now, man, but you've got to be part of this. We're counting on you."

Zack heard what Adam said, and saw Ben close his eyes as if he were in pain.

"Francesca didn't seem so happy that you took off," Adam added, loud enough for everyone to hear. "She waited around for a while. You could tell she was looking for you."

Every muscle in Ben's body tightened. Then, without saying a word, he picked up his guitar and headed for the exit. Zack phoned his mother, while Carly and Kevin grabbed the rest of Ben's gear. They waited in the parking lot in silence.

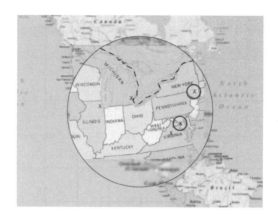

CHAPTER TWENTY-SIX

X'S AND O'S

Zack

Saturday morning, the smell of breakfast drew the four of them to the dining room table. Aunt Tina was sure to serve Sharon and herself before the kids even sat down.

"Aunt Tina, this is great," Carly said.

"Mm-hmm." The others agreed, nodding with their mouths full.

"You kids are eating machines." She laughed, watching them.

Zack put down his fork. "Mom, can we go to the movies later?"

"Yes," she replied. "Make it an early one; I want you home before dinner."

++++++++++

After breakfast, they went straight to the guesthouse. Carly sat in front of the computer with her fingers on the keyboard. It was rare for anyone other than Kevin to occupy that seat, but he was at the kitchen table examining the maps. He sat with the large corkboard propped up at his side, while his eyes were on his tablet.

"If we're going to take the coin to the Library of Congress, we should do it soon," Zack said, checking his phone for the time.

"I hate turning that penny over to someone. It might take us back to the barn if we keep it," Carly said.

"Mr. Thomas told us we had to turn the coin over to Mr. Jefferson," Kevin chimed from the kitchen.

"Yeah, he might know something that can help us. Plus, it does no good if we keep seeing Dad and Bill, but can't get to them," Ben said.

"I guess you're right," Carly conceded. Her eyes went back to the monitor. "Here it is. 'Harold Frederick was a lobbyist in the 1950s,'" she read out loud. "'He was an advocate for the automotive industry as well as the television broadcasting industry.'"

"Notice both could pay big money," Zack added.

"You can't slight the man for doing his job," Ben defended. "Lobbyists are supposed to get politicians to pass laws that are good for their clients. Every special interest group has someone lobbying for them in Washington."

"That guy was a crook. He may have done right by his client, but what he did was illegal. He should have ended up in jail right next to Shorty," Zack insisted.

"'Mr. Frederick died in 1965,'" Carly continued reading. "'Survived by one sister and a nephew.'"

"He mentioned his nephew, remember?" Kevin called out.

"He also said that a guy at Ford might like one of the coins." Ben looked over at Zack. "He must have been talking about the Ford Motor Company, right?"

"Yeah, the guy at Ford and the nephew are who we'll target next," Zack stated.

"That's all there is on Frederick," Carly said with a slight smile. "But I did find something here on Earl."

"What?" Ben asked.

"It appears that our Earl became a congressman for the state of Virginia. He relinquished his seat at the end of last year because of an illness, but it doesn't say what the illness was. He must still be alive or there would be something here about his death."

"He would be in his seventies by now," Zack calculated.

"We couldn't have found the coin and would have no leads on the others if it wasn't for Earl," Carly stated.

"I never asked—what was in the envelope you gave him?" Ben said.

"Five hundred dollars and a card expressing our appreciation."

"Wow, you went through a lot of money this week," Zack said.

"All of that money in the safe does no one any good just sitting there. Actually, for what we got in return, I would say it was a bargain," Carly concluded.

"Guys, come in here. I need some help," Kevin called to them.

When they entered the small kitchen, Zack noticed two maps that he had never seen before pinned to the corkboard. "What's this?"

"Things are starting to make sense," Kevin said. "We've been looking at these maps all wrong. I think I found what ties them together."

"Let's hear it," Zack said as he, Ben, and Carly took a seat around the table.

"When I was doing a search on 1943 copper pennies, I found a record of sale for one of them," Kevin said. "These coins are so rare that every time they've changed hands, it's documented. After I found two more, I thought it was weird that all three of the sales took place in cities where we have maps. Since then, I've been looking for more sales records."

"I don't think there would be a record of every time Dad and Sam got one of the coins," Zack said, dismissing the idea.

"That's not what I mean," Kevin responded. "The ones I've found listed the person's name, place, and date the coin was purchased. I think Dad and Sam were using this information to track down the coins."

"Now that would totally make sense," Ben said. He looked at Zack and they both nodded.

"Help me do this and we'll see if I'm right," Kevin said. "What I need for you guys to do is separate the maps."

"How many in each stack?" Ben asked, already taking some of the maps, while Zack and Carly divided up the rest.

"Not like that," Kevin directed. "I want you to separate them by area. First find the cities in Greece."

They each searched through their pile of maps.

"Thessaloniki is mine," Carly announced.

"Here's Athens," Zack said.

"We've been looking at these maps separately," Kevin said. "What I'm thinking is that the maps for cities that are close to each other should be put together and counted as one area."

Zack and Ben looked at each other and shrugged their shoulders.

"Maybe," Zack said.

Kevin picked up a blue marker and turned to the new maps he had pinned on the board. He placed a blue X over Greece. "Next, I need London and Cambridge, United Kingdom."

"Got both," Ben said.

Kevin continued to call out areas while the others pulled the maps from their piles.

"Okay, there will be only one map per area for the rest of the cities."

"Detroit, Michigan."

"Me," Carly stated. Kevin put a blue X on Detroit.

"Charlottesville, Virginia," Kevin called.

"Okay," Ben said, pulling out the Charlottesville map.

"Chicago, Illinois."

"Mine," Ben responded.

"Washington, DC," Kevin said.

"That's mine." Zack motioned.

"All right, that should be it," Kevin stated.

"I still have Bora Bora," Carly told him.

"It's definitely on the list. I must have skipped that one." Kevin looked for the small island on the map to place an *X*.

"Do you guys have any maps left?" Kevin asked Zack and Ben.

"Nothing."

"Good," Kevin said. "It's taken me a while to track down the records of sale. I just found another one, which gives me eight locations. So, let's see if I'm right." He took the piece of paper with a list of his findings along with a red marker and turned to the maps. "The first recorded sale of a 1943 copper penny was in 1958 in San Francisco." He drew a red circle around the X on San Francisco. "Kingston," he announced, as he circled New York.

He continued to circle the areas that corresponded with his list of sales transactions. The others watched as he marked the maps, and Zack knew Kevin was right. When he finished, there were four blue *X*'s that remained with no red circle around them.

"That leaves Charlottesville, Detroit, Chicago, and Washington, DC," Kevin said.

"Kevin, you're a genius," Zack told him. He knew Kevin didn't like being referred to as a genius, but coming from him, he was sure Kevin would gladly take it.

"Good going, Kevin," Ben remarked.

"So, if I'm getting this right, you can circle DC," Carly said. "There was no recorded sale, but that's where we got the coin from Shorty."

"That's right," Kevin said, placing a red circle around the blue X on Washington, DC. "That makes nine coins, plus The Lincoln makes ten. Our grandfather already had The Lincoln, so there wouldn't be a map to search for that penny."

"But there would still be a record of the sale," Zack pointed out.

"If there is I couldn't find it. There wasn't one 1943 copper penny recorded as sold in 1962," Kevin said.

"But that's when Dad said Grandfather bought it," Zack insisted.

"I know, but we still have maps for Detroit, Chicago, and Charlottesville, and there weren't sales records for them either," Kevin said. "Our dads must have thought the coins were somewhere in these cities, or why else would they have these maps?"

"I think you're right," Ben said. "With eight coins recorded as being purchased in eight of the exact areas of our maps, plus the one we got in DC, I think it's safe to say that the last two lost coins are in Detroit, Chicago, or Charlottesville.

"Yeah," Kevin agreed. "Those are the only maps we need to be looking at. The problem is there are three city maps, but only two coins left to find. I don't know what the third map is for."

"Kevin, maybe you really are a genius," Zack congratulated him once again.

"The thing is," Kevin said, ignoring his brother's comment. "Now we know where to look, but we don't know what year."

"How are we going to figure that out?" Zack asked.

"No idea," Kevin said.

Ben looked at the time on his phone. "We'd better get going if we're taking this coin to the library," he said.

"I still don't feel good about giving the coin up," Carly said.

"What is it that you *do* feel good about?" Zack snapped as he walked out of the guesthouse to tell his mother they were leaving.

Carly's eyes narrowed as she stared at the door closing behind him.

Kevin pulled out the GPS and began turning the knob, inputting the address of the Library of Congress. Zack joined them at their bikes and they once again headed for the lookout. They pumped their bikes up the trail and reached Topanga Canyon Boulevard. The street was unusually clear, and after making it across, they pushed their bikes deep into the bushes. Zack placed The Lincoln into the GPS. He held it out for the others to grab hold of the handle.

"Make sure your wristbands are secure," Kevin warned before pushing the button.

The iridescent purple line poured around them like liquid, and the electromagnetic field encapsulated them in complete silence. They all hoped to see their fathers, but after only a second, they fell to the ground.

CHAPTER TWENTY-SEVEN

MR. POSTMAN

Zack

"Where are we?" Kevin asked as they found themselves surrounded by large shrubs instead of pine trees.

"I think we're at the Lincoln Memorial. They must have replaced the trees with bushes," Carly said, getting up and peering out from the seclusion of the shrubs, confirming that they had landed in the same place as their previous trips.

From the moment they made their way from between the bushes, they were struck by the contrast from fifty years ago. The cars and signs all looked like things they would see in their everyday lives.

"It feels weird being here in our normal clothes," Carly said.

"I know," Kevin agreed. "At least we don't have to worry about fitting in."

They made their way to the parking lot, where the public transportation was lined up in the same way it had been in the 1950s. They slipped into a cab and were all a little surprised when they arrived at the library and the driver announced that the fare was $11.95. A far cry from the seventy-five cents they had paid before.

The Library of Congress looked the same, although it was now surrounded by buildings nearly the size of the library itself. They climbed the stairs and, as they got closer, were alarmed at the changes made to the carriage entrance. There was now a security checkpoint.

Zack handed Ben the coin they planned to return. "If they won't let me through security with the GPS, take the coin to Mr. Thomas and I'll wait for you guys right outside this door," Zack told him.

A sign reading "ENTRANCE FOR RESERVED TOURS, PROFESSIONAL APPOINTMENTS, RESEARCHERS AND WHEELCHAIRS" was posted next to the entrance. Zack quickly got behind the last person of a group filing through security, and the others followed. The GPS and backpack made it through with no problem. Carly and Kevin were also allowed through, but Zack and Ben both set off the metal detector's alarm. The guard ushered them to the side and asked to view the contents of their pockets. The each showed the guard their penny, and handed the coins to Carly before walking through the sensors again. No sound followed, and they were cleared to enter the building. Carly returned the coins to them, and they approached the information desk.

"We are here to see Mr. Jefferson," Carly said to the young man behind the desk.

"Let me see if he's in his office," he replied. He typed something into his computer, and after a moment, got to his feet.

"Right this way." He gestured for them to follow. "Please wait in here," he said as he opened a door.

It was not the same room they had been in fifty years earlier, but it was nearly identical.

Carly shivered. "It's freezing in here." She folded her arms around herself and took a seat.

After only a short wait, a man entered the room. His dyed black hair was slicked back and his pitted skin had an unnatural sheen to it. He was wearing jeans and a sport coat, seeming to be trying a bit too hard to look casual. Zack already didn't like him. There was something about the man that made him think of Baumgart.

Without introducing himself or asking their names, the man went straight to business.

"It's a surprise to have you here," he announced in a deep voice as he sat down behind the desk. "Where are your fathers?"

"They've been kidnapped," Zack stated.

"I am well aware of that, but how did the power of the twelfth coin transfer to you?" the man asked.

"We aren't exactly sure how the coin came to us, but it did, and we figured out how to use it," Zack said, giving as few details as possible.

"How did you know to come here?" Mr. Jefferson asked with a tone of suspicion.

"The coin took us back to 1954, where we met Mr. Thomas. He explained our dads' quest and told us to come to you with any coins that we find," Zack said.

Mr. Jefferson appraised each of them as a distasteful expression formed on his face.

"We have come to turn in the coin, and ask if you know where our dads are," Zack continued.

The look on the man's face changed, and there was a sudden gleam in his eye. "You have made the right decision," he said. "I'm in charge of the security and recovery of the missing coins. Your fathers have disregarded protocol many times since I've taken this post. They have continually ignored my request to notify me prior to using the coin that they refer to as The Lincoln," he stated, getting worked up as he spoke.

He paused for a moment and took a deep breath. His tone turned sugary sweet. "Their secrecy may have cost them their lives. At least we won't have to worry about that with you, will we? You are doing the right thing by giving me the twelfth coin. There's no need for you to put yourselves in such danger. I will continue the search for the remaining three coins, and of course your fathers," he added as an afterthought.

"What?" Zack questioned, taken aback by what Mr. Jefferson was saying. "We aren't giving you The Lincoln. The coin we have brought here is one of the missing coins."

Mr. Jefferson's eyebrows rose, emphasizing the wrinkles across his forehead. "You have recovered one of the three remaining lost coins?" he asked in disbelief.

"Yeah," Zack replied.

"Hmmm." The man cupped his chin in his hand and took a moment before continuing, still seeming unconvinced. "Men have searched for years to no avail for the last three coins. How exactly were you able to retrieve one of them?"

Zack was leery of revealing too much. The others continued to let him take the lead in the conversation and remained silent.

"Does that matter?" Zack questioned.

Mr. Jefferson looked irritated by Zack's answer.

"Unlike my predecessors, I am active in the search for the coins," the man spouted. "Only two have held this position before me. Which one of those did you say you spoke with? Would that have been the fool that lost the coins to begin with?"

"He didn't lose them," Zack defended.

"You do not know the truth surrounding the theft of the coins," the man asserted.

"Really? Why don't you tell us?" Zack said, glancing at the others, who were nodding.

"That is classified information," the man replied.

"If we decide not to give you this coin—" Zack began.

Mr. Jefferson quickly stood with his fists clenched. He put his knuckles on the desk and leaned toward them. "You do not have that choice!" he yelled, having lost his patience. "The contract drawn up between your grandfather and this office states he and his heirs will be allowed to retain the twelfth coin for the sole purpose of continuing the search for the coins that remain missing. Each coin must be returned to this office as they are found." He continued his rant. "Any breech of this agreement and all coins in your possession must be returned to me immediately, at which time the agreement will be dissolved." He shook his head. "The thought of allowing civilians to undertake this high-security mission is ludicrous. These decisions were made before I was assigned this position, or you can be assured neither you nor any member of your family would have been allowed to lay a finger on the twelfth coin."

"Is that a threat?" Ben spoke for the first time since the man entered the room.

Mr. Jefferson took a deliberate breath and spoke in a low, controlled voice as he returned to his seat. "Who knows you're here right now?" he asked as his eyes traveled over each of them.

They returned his stare and didn't respond.

"As I suspected." He glared at Zack. "I'm sure that one phone conversation with your mother would prevent you from finding any more coins and continuing the search for your fathers." He looked at Ben, then back at Zack. "So, don't come here with some teenage know-it-all attitude, because I'll set you straight in a hurry."

"We're out of here," Zack announced. They stood to leave, and Ben placed the coin on the desk.

"If you fall upon either of the two remaining coins, remember the agreement. The coins must be returned to me at this office."

"Let's go," Ben prompted, and they walked out.

"What a jerk," Kevin said as they moved down the hall toward the exit.

"That must be some binding agreement made by your grandfather," Ben said. "The man wants The Lincoln bad—you could see it on his face. He looked like he was ready to fight you for it when you said you weren't giving it to him."

Still in disbelief over what they'd just experienced, they looked for an area where they could depart unnoticed. The building across the street that hadn't been there on their previous visits offered the shelter they needed. Zack pulled out the GPS and handed it to Kevin.

"That guy's definitely not going to help us find our dads," Ben said.

"That's for sure! I don't trust him," Zack added as he watched Kevin toggle through the letters and numbers.

"I don't think it's him we have to worry about right now," Carly said.

"Meaning?" Zack questioned.

"You heard what those guys in the barn said. They are coming after us, and your mom."

Kevin held out the GPS and everyone gripped the handle. He pushed the button, and their shoulders raised as they cringed in reaction to the shrieking high-pitched sound that pained their ears. The protective layer formed around them, and the ground fell away from their feet as they began to spin. A moment later, they dropped to the ground.

++++++++++

They heard the sound of passing cars and knew they were in Topanga Canyon. Ben was first to the bikes, pulling them from the shrubs. It took a while before they were able to cross the street, but once they did, they followed the path leading home.

"They've been gone for almost two weeks," Carly said with concern as they rode. "We're running out of time."

"You're right, we'll look every day till we find them," Ben promised.

"We're going to have to watch out for ourselves and keep a close eye on Mom," Zack said, nodding to Kevin as they rode off of the trail onto the cul-de-sac.

"How are we supposed to do that while we're at school?" Kevin questioned.

"I don't know, but we'd better figure something out," Zack said as they rode up the driveway.

They leaned their bikes against the garage and went up to the main house. Kevin opened the door to find Sharon in the kitchen.

"Hi, Mom," Kevin said as he entered with the others following.

"Hi, honey, you're back awfully early."

"Where's Aunt Tina?" he asked, looking around.

"You just missed her. She's coming back on Tuesday and staying the rest of the week."

"That solves that problem," Zack mumbled.

"Zack, would you go down to the mailbox? I forgot to check it yesterday," Sharon said as she fingered through a small stack of carry-out menus.

"Why does our mailbox have to be down at the stupid curb?" he complained.

"Just do what I asked, please," she replied.

"Yes, Mother," he mocked, walking out of the house.

Everyone else's mailbox is next to their front door, so why does ours have to be at the street? He walked to the end of the driveway and approached the box. Irritated at the inconvenience, he yanked open the mailbox door and looked inside. There was one letter propped upright. The white envelope displayed no address or postage, only the name Zack Marshall scribbled across the front.

He looked back at the house and saw that the door was closed. Glancing around, he noticed nothing out of the ordinary. Examining the envelope more closely, he felt something inside. He carefully unstuck the flap and poured the contents into his hand. His stomach sank as he recognized the chain from his dad's pocket watch. He looked around again, but saw nothing unusual. Unable to wait, he removed the paper inside.

He carefully unfolded it and read.

*Job well done! Find the two remaining coins and
I will exchange
your fathers for them. Do it quickly while
they are still alive!*

A shot of fear coursed through his body, and he felt as though he was going to be sick. He leaned back against the mailbox, clutching the note. After a few moments, he knew what must be done. He shoved the note into his pocket and headed for the house.

EPILOGUE

Virginia, March 1943

Hanford felt every year of his age as he held his chest, trying to catch his breath. He glanced back down from the bell tower stairs he had just climbed. "What is it that you had to show me?" he asked the man who had convinced him to go up there.

"This beautiful view to start with," his companion replied, moving closer to the edge of the platform and gesturing for the old man to do the same.

Hanford didn't move. "You told me that this had something to do with the coins."

"Oh, come on, Hanford," his companion said. "Come closer and you'll see what I mean." He held his hand out.

Hanford was hesitant, but slowly shuffled forward. He looked out, but could barely see through the morning fog. "Stop this nonsense," the old man demanded. "What is the reason you insisted I follow you up here?"

"I told you, it's about the coins," his companion replied calmly.

"Well then, get on with it," Hanford pressed.

"Last week, in the generator room, you witnessed the culmination of years of my hard work." The man's lips tightened and his voice rose. "My confidential findings were revealed like they were common knowledge."

The agitation in his companion's voice was obvious, and Hanford's eyes went to the stairs. "I'm going back down," he announced.

"No you're not!" He grabbed the old man's arm.

"Then get to the point," Hanford snapped, pulling his arm from the man's grasp.

"The point is that no one asked my permission to share the secrets of my discoveries."

"Your secrets are safe with me. I'll take them to my grave," Hanford promised.

"Which will be sooner than you think," his companion told him. With one swift move, the two men stood face-to-face.

"What are you doing?"

"I'm keeping you to your word," the man replied, grabbing Hanford by the lapels of his coat and jerking him closer to the edge of the platform.

"Let go of me!" Hanford insisted, seeing the menacing look on the man's face.

"As you wish," his companion replied. He let go of Hanford's coat and gave him a hard shove.

"NO!" Hanford yelled. The toes of his shoes gripped the last inch of the platform, and his arms swung around like a windmill. He tried to keep his balance, but it was futile. "NOOOO," he screamed as his body went over the edge. His voice echoed through the empty streets, only to be silenced by the thud of his body hitting the ground.

++++++++++

That evening…

Rain beat the ivy creeping up the side of the building. The scalloped edges of the awning swung back and forth in the wind, offering no protection to the club member who rushed under it. The man hurried past the doorman, stopping just inside to wipe his feet on the rug.

"Good evening, Mr. Cannon," the attendant said, extending his hand for the man's sopping coat and hat. "He's waiting for you in the conference room."

The man nodded and, taking the stairs two at a time, he headed down the hallway of Randolph Manor, a spacious two-story home now converted to serve as a private place where government officials and businessmen could meet away from the public eye. He approached the conference room and tapped on the closed door before entering to see a long table with only one chair occupied.

"Carl," he said. "This better be good to have me out in this storm."

"Ah, George, thank you for coming," Carl replied, standing to shake George's hand. "Take a seat. I wouldn't have asked you here if it weren't important."

"Everything seems to be important these days," George remarked, pulling out a chair.

A butler entered the room carrying a tray laden with glasses of ice floating in an amber liquid. He placed a drink near George and traded Carl's empty glass for a full one before leaving the room.

"Now, what is it that couldn't wait till morning?" George asked.

"Hanford has been murdered," Carl stated.

"Another one?" George couldn't believe it.

It had been only one week since the coins were pressed, and nine out of the eleven men who took part in the project were dead. George felt a flash of guilt. He was the one who'd assembled the genius group, stressing their obligation in keeping the United States safe.

"That's right," Carl replied. Gulping down half of his drink, he slammed his glass on the table. "Have these murders been your men's doing?"

"No!" George spouted in defense. "It wouldn't benefit us to take the lives of this country's greatest minds."

"The president is demanding to know the extent of our involvement," Carl stated.

"I met with both Miller and Professor Osborne over three months ago and explained the nuclear threat that we were facing," George said.

"Yes, I read that in your report, but you failed to mention how you were able to convince Osborne to hand over his technology."

"When Osborne saw Thurman Miller get run down right in front of him, he was terrified. He accused me of having arranged the killing, and I didn't deny it."

"But you said—" Carl started.

George's hand went up. "My men had nothing to do with the murder. But at the time, I couldn't have bought better leverage. Osborne was scared to death and offered to give up all that he had developed if I would allow him to complete his study."

"He could drag that out forever," Carl remarked.

"That's precisely why I helped fast-track his endeavor," George said. "I appealed to some of those involved in the Manhattan Project, most of whom had heard rumors of Osborne's advancements. When I told them of the plan to use his technology as a safeguard against a nuclear attack on the United States, they all agreed to participate. So, the ten of them, and Professor Osborne, had a few meetings. The next thing I knew, we were watching the professor's assistant pouring copper into molds."

"Your telling me they've succeeded?" Carl asked.

"Not quite yet. The tests haven't gone perfectly. But the professor and his assistant have made some adjustments, and tomorrow I'm allowing them to use the master coin to try again. The professor has assured me that it will work this time."

"Why haven't you brought me this information?"

"I was waiting for the tests to be completed," George replied.

"If the professor is right and it works, I'll arrange a meeting with the president," Carl said. "He has his hands full right now, but you should turn the coins over to him directly."

"It sounds outlandish to say that a means of time travel has been developed that's strong enough to take this country back in time to erase any devastation that someone might force upon us, but that's exactly what we'll have," George told him.

"Just make sure you are not making false promises, especially to the president of the United States."

George nodded.

"Have you any suspects in the murders?" Carl asked, draining his glass.

"We're still working on it, but we believe it's one individual."

"Only two of the men involved in creating the coins are still alive. Put your entire team on finding the murderer. Use whatever resources it takes. The killer must be stopped."

END OF BOOK ONE

Connect with us at thetwelfthcoin.com
for series updates and prizes.

About the Author

With the flu, bedtime came early. That's when the feverish dream began. Three teens—two boys and a girl—were walking down an alley alongside a younger boy on a bike. Just ahead of them, a small spot on the ground began to glow. Suddenly a bright light flooded the area, and colored beams shot out in every direction. While shafts of light crisscrossed through the air, a blue beam held steady in front of one of the boys. Mesmerized by the light, he watched as mathematical equations formed above the beam and floated toward him. As if in a trance he nodded, repeating the only word that he could force from his lips, "Yes." Suddenly the lights were gone. They rushed to the spot to see what appeared to be an ordinary penny. The dream ended, but the vivid images replayed throughout the night.

The following morning, Kimberly Erjavac became a writer.

The Twelfth Coin is Kimberly's first series of novels. Born in Detroit and raised in Ecorse and Woodhaven, Michigan, she now resides in Los Angeles.